THE FINAL PROGRAMME

Also available from Michael Moorcock,
Titan Books and Titan Comics

A NOMAD OF THE TIME STREAMS

The Warlord of the Air
The Land Leviathan
The Steel Tsar

THE ETERNAL CHAMPION SERIES

The Eternal Champion
Phoenix in Obsidian
The Dragon in the Sword

THE CORUM SERIES

The Knight of the Swords
The Queen of the Swords
The King of the Swords
The Bull and the Spear
The Oak and the Ram
The Sword and the Stallion

THE CORNELIUS QUARTET

A Cure for Cancer (March 2016)
The English Assassin (April 2016)
The Condition of Muzak (May 2016)

THE MICHAEL MOORCOCK LIBRARY

Elric of Melniboné
Elric: Sailor on the Seas of Fate

MICHAEL MOORCOCK'S ELRIC

Volume 1: The Ruby Throne
Volume 2: Stormbringer

MICHAEL MOORCOCK

THE FINAL PROGRAMME

THE CORNELIUS QUARTET

TITAN BOOKS

The Final Programme
Print edition ISBN: 9781783291779
E-book edition ISBN: 9781783291762

Published by Titan Books
A division of Titan Publishing Group Ltd
144 Southwark Street, London SE1 0UP

First Titan edition: February 2016
1 2 3 4 5 6 7 8 9 10

Edited by John Davey.

A CIP catalogue record for this title is available from the British Library.

Printed and bound in the United States

THE FINAL PROGRAMME

Illustrated by Malcolm Dean

Additional illustrations by Harry Douthwaite

For Alfred Bester

CONTENTS

THE REPOSSESSION OF JERRY CORNELIUS

by John Clute

Once upon a time a rather unremarkable composer and music publisher named Anton Diabelli composed a rather unremarkable waltz—simple to hum and easy to remember—and then he had an idea. As he was always looking for material to publish, especially music that could be played by amateurs on the piano, why not (he thought) take this waltz around to as many composers as possible (eventually he found fifty of them) and have them each write a variation on the thing? Then he could put the fifty-one pieces into what was commonly called (at this time, 1823) a *pasticcio*, a collection of works by various hands, all in the style of some original composer, and then hawk his *pasticcio* far and wide. Which is more or less what happened. But what if Diabelli had been a trickier, more formidable composer? What if he had given his fifty composers not the simple-hearted waltz history records, but only a variation of the *real tune*?

Rather more recently, in January 1965, a young writer and author named Michael Moorcock, who seemed rather unremarkable at the time, composed a regular waltz of a novel called *The Final Programme*, excerpts from which caused some comment when published soon after in NEW WORLDS, the SF magazine he had then been editing for about half a year. Easy to read, linearly plotted, full of SF twists and turns, this novel introduced to the SF world (and in fact seemed to donate to some of its writers) a new kind of infinitely malleable template for myth-making called Jerry Cornelius, simple to hum and easy to remember, a sexually ambivalent, amoral (but exceedingly oral) portmanteau anti-hero who was part saint and part devil, an instant myth of the pop sixties whose tastes in music, clothes, cars, drugs, wombs, technology and apotheosis all seemed to make him an authentic emblem of Swinging London and (more narrowly) of the New Wave in SF which Moorcock had instigated by giving space to its writers in his magazine, which soon became notorious. As did its mascot. Moorcock encouraged his fellow writers to use Cornelius as a template in stories of their own. There may not have been fifty of them, and NEW WORLDS hardly became a *pasticcio*, but all the same it was pretty clear—indeed advertised—that *The Final Programme* was being used, sometimes very competently, as the initial theme for a whole series of mythopoeic variations, whole multiverses of riffs, on Jerry himself; on Miss Brunner, his collaborator in instant Messiah-hood; on Frank, his shifty, scrounging brother; and on Catherine, the sister he's deeply in love with.

But what if *The Final Programme* turned out not to

be the basic template tune at all? What if it was only a variation on the real tune?

The fate of Diabelli's theme is well known, for the poor devil had the singular luck to approach Ludwig van Beethoven with his little template waltz. Sick, deaf, and ageing, the great composer slammed the door in his face at first, but later, somehow intrigued by the tune, he told Diabelli that he would undertake the task after all. He then exceeded his brief; instead of one variation he wrote thirty-three— they comprise his final and perhaps greatest work for solo piano. They last an hour. You could call them the real tune.

What happened with Michael Moorcock is rather different. After seeming to give Jerry Cornelius to the world as a pop saviour, he turned and took him back, just as though he were Diabelli and Beethoven both, in one skin. The final result, all thirty-three variations, became the four central Cornelius volumes now known as *The Cornelius Quartet*: *The Final Programme* (1968); *A Cure for Cancer* (1971); *The English Assassin* (1972) and *The Condition of Muzak* (1977). Being published over such a long span, these volumes may have initially given off a sense of improvisation; but in fact they read best when understood as a single sustained novel. Moreover, like most books whose structure is most easily described in musical terms, the meaning of *The Cornelius Quartet* only comes clear as the end is neared. What may have seemed, in the first instalment, to be the main theme turns out, in the end, to have been a variation; only as *The Condition of Muzak* reaches apotheosis do we hear the real tune in its entirety.

That basic theme—it is Jerry Cornelius's fundamental obsessive concern through all his various incarnations—is easy to put but hard to play: because authenticity in the city is a costume drama, how can any late-twentieth-century city dweller acquire and maintain an identity strategically capable of constituting urban life?

The presentation of self in everyday life in the inner city is a form of theatre, where identity is rôle and where entropy is high, for time is passing. Jerry Cornelius is the paradigmatic native of the inner city; his rôles constitute a genuine paradigm set of strategies for living there. His inner city is London (but could be New York), his patch is Ladbroke Grove. His real story (I believe) runs from about 1965 to about a decade later, a period during which London had been destroying itself as a place to live, hence the rapacity of his need for safety and solace. It is for this reason that the various masquerades and venues which make up his story read as a series of precariously achieved enclaves, or wombs. To shift the metaphor, Jerry's life is a constant series of *auditions*. His constant failures are the failures of the city (circa 1975) where ultimately there are no enclaves, no permanent wombs, for time rots them. No music stays fresh. Jonathan Raban speaks to something of the same general point in his socio-literary study of the meaning of urban life, *Soft City* (1974):

> Sociology and anthropology are not disciplines
> which take easily to situations where people are able

to live out their fantasies, not just in the symbolic action of ritual, but in the concrete theatre of society at large. The city is one such situation. Its conditions effectively break down many of the conventional distinctions between dream life and real life; the city inside the head can be transformed, with the aid of the technology of style, into the city on the streets. To a very large degree, people can create their cosmologies at will, liberating themselves from the deterministic schemes which ought to have led them into a wholly different style of life. To have a platonic conception of oneself, and to make it spring forth, fully clothed, out of one's head, is one of the most dangerous and essential city freedoms, and it is a freedom which has been ignored and underestimated by almost everyone except novelists.

Michael Moorcock is one of those novelists. His main gloss on Raban may be that the city in our time being deeply entropic, life within it therefore tends to the condition of Muzak.

But he's also an SF writer, and the whole of *The Final Programme* is sparkling good SF. Being the most extended single riff on the basic theme of identity maintenance in the entire tetralogy, it is consequently the most easily assimilated story, very remote from the darker, more complex, virtually Edwardian verisimilitude of later pages, grimmer times. *The Final Programme* is a constitutive image of the sunshine of surviving at a time (1965) when (perhaps for Moorcock, too)

London bore an air of slightly pixillated ebullience. London swung. The story reflects this. Jerry and Miss Brunner (here, a computer technician with enormous powers—it's only in the final book that she's revealed for what she always was in the city, a tight-assed schoolmarm from Ladbroke Grove) clash and conspire from here to Lapland and Angkor Wat (to be similarly grounded as a dream of Derry & Toms department store half-choked in its own overgrown roof garden), and eventually get their computers and their super-science formulae together in a womblike cave where they merge themselves into a new hermaphrodite Messiah for whom the world is "tasty", so it eats the world.

Altogether there's a lot of vampirism in both *The Final Programme* and succeeding parts of the tetralogy; part of the time it's an SF energy-transfer, a countervailing response to the loss of usable energy in this venue or that; ultimately it reads as an analogue of the use people make of each others' images (or life-forces) in coping with the interplay of dramaturgies that constitutes social life in the deep city. In any case, Jerry Cornelius as polymorphous Messiah could be said to constitute the false theme of the tetralogy, the spunky little Diabelli waltz; for though it makes a nice story (and helped fuel the New Wave's own wry messianism), generally speaking Jerry is anything but…

In A *Cure for Cancer*, which is a kind of negative scherzo on the pattern of the first book, he has polarised into a black with white hair, and continues to vampirise those about him to maintain his own image-stability. A couple of years have passed in the real world; the scene has darkened, witness the headlines and news reports and arms advertisements that appear more and more frequently in the text and whose function is not to make editorial points about the world (they'd date very quickly), but to demonstrate some of the ways in which the world acts as a shaping, controlling input on its victims (us, Jerry); headlines are like executive memos in the Castle. War has come, American "advisors" have turned Europe into something very like the news reports of life in Vietnam. We are inundated with media. Jerry Cornelius makes to dance in step, to keep alive, to recover his beloved sister. He runs a transmogrification service which forcibly does to others what the media do to all of us, thus maintaining a kind of intricate balance. He goes to a strange America (perhaps Kafka's) continuing a conflict with the newly introduced, loathsome Bishop Beesley, who with Miss Brunner seems to represent the only kind of officialdom Moorcock is willing to deal with directly; their life-denying "orderliness" constantly threatens Jerry's identity and the enclaves of aesthetic harmony he and his compatriots try to inhabit.

We meet most of these compatriots in the next volume, *The English Assassin*, where the action broadens and deepens significantly. We are into the 1970s in the city, and Jerry has retreated very far indeed within the action. Having gone into a fugue of horror at the collapse of the century, he spends most of the novel in a coffin, beneath the surface of the newly ornate narrative, whose Edwardian cadences depict a turn-of-the-century dream of the romance of Empire at its hectic Jubilee peak. *The English Assassin* is also full of nostalgia for

Edwardian visions of what the future might hold, dreams of a time when art nouveau flying boats and zeppelins would criss-cross a balkanised Europe with *fin-de-siècle* lords and ladies, a time when all the weapons and appurtenances of technological progress would make up a glorious raree-show. Every single invention would be fixed still in time long enough to be memorised, the great Duesenberg would not turn to junk before we had a chance to make a symbol of it, every surface of the steam yacht would be polished and legible and reflect our faces. Into these scenes of nostalgia for an endurable future are introduced various lords and ladies, the tetralogy's remaining important characters, who dance out their rôles on Jerry's coffin: Sebastian Auckinek, the two Nyes (Captain and Major), Colonel Pyat, Prinz Lobkowitz, and most importantly Una Persson (stage singer and dancer, revolutionary, Catherine's lover and Jerry's) and Mrs Cornelius (his appallingly greedy, vulgar, foul-mouthed libidinous mother, who seems to represent an earlier form of city life—a sly, savage, indomitable, wise Cockney survivor of everything the century can throw at her). These lords and ladies are alive in their own right, but also represent Jerry's desperate attempts to apply fixative to the Empire and to time, so as to maintain himself in a lousy era.

Of course it doesn't work. The Edwardian vision of Empire is deeply tubercular; the Edwardian dreams of the future are hopelessly innocent, hopelessly pre-war. The bright clothing and the jamborees rot, like Jerry in his coffin. The entropic decay of the British Empire mirrors the entropic decay of Jerry's attempts at constituting images of survival in dehumanised London as the sixties turn sourly downwards into the seventies. A dozen futures have died for us SF readers before we could breathe them to life. Golems stalk the council flats. *The English Assassin* ends in fire and death. There is a lot of ageing going on: it's the nature of the catastrophe.

And so we reach *The Condition of Muzak*, which repossesses Jerry Cornelius from messiah-hood and other intoxications by retelling his earlier lives in its own complex terms, as phases in a harlequinade. In *The Final Programme* and *A Cure for Cancer* Jerry has seemed to be Harlequin himself, the dominant figure of all the show, manipulating costumes and plot at will so as to reach a point of stable bliss with Columbine, who is his sister Catherine. He snaps his fingers at incest, and the world shrivels at his dancing feet. But of course it doesn't work. In *The English Assassin* he has gone to earth, and as we reach the dense heart of *The Condition of Muzak* (the chapters leading up to his final Ladbroke Grove party, which this time is a genuine masquerade) we find him undergoing a strange metamorphosis. He is deeply withdrawn (therefore London is deserted), but manages to struggle back to the roof garden at Derry & Toms as to a tropical womb, where he settles into a foetal position and, umbilically tied by earphones to music emblematic of his past lives, sinks into near coma, which is no way for Harlequin to act. The whole department store is covered with roots and vines and undergrowth, but finally Major Nye and Hythloday (the Professor Hira of *The Final Programme*, whose first meeting with Jerry thus anticipates his last) discover Jerry and drag him to safety in a nearby house, where he lapses into catatonia, only to be ultimately aroused, and reborn, as Pierrot. It must be a great relief. Deep within he has always been incapable of the coercive manipulations his rôles as Harlequin have laid on him. Deep within he has always really been Pierrot the Weeper, helplessly in love with Columbine, and always at risk of losing her to the genuine Harlequin, who is Una Persson.

Indeed, everyone is relieved. There is a fugue of joy. Though Jerry is only a figurehead now, the Empire in all its parti-coloured glory returns to honour him as the King of London in a coronation parade lasting hours in the bright sun. The dream of Empire has come true. Time passes in this dream. Christmas is nigh. Over the course of an extraordinary sequence that marries Dickens and Wells in a description of a London heartbreakingly clement and legible as the snow falls and everyone sings carols, Harlequin leads us through gaily bedizened streets to the Ladbroke Grove party, whose zone of peace has spread this time throughout the town. Jerry is there as Pierrot, Catherine as Columbine is in a magic sleep, Harlequin awakens her lovingly (Una Persson loves Catherine too), but gives her up to Pierrot. In a London prepared to rejoice with him at such a moment, Jerry Cornelius has won his heart's desire.

But of course it doesn't work.

Framing the rest of *The Condition of Muzak* are several chapters of another complexion entirely, also set in the Ladbroke Grove area of London, Jerry's mythical home, but no longer is Ladbroke Grove mythical. Jerry Cornelius is a teenager who lives with his gluttonous mother and his seedy brother Frank in a slum flat. He is rather seedy himself. He spends much of his time in a "tiny balcony formed by the house's front porch", which he plans to turn someday into "an ornamental conservatory with semi-tropical plants", and suddenly we realise with a sort of horror that this imaginary conservatory grounds the roof garden at Derry & Toms in the same way that that roof garden grounds most of the exotic locations (like Angkor Wat) of the entire tetralogy. It is a shocking discovery. Jerry Cornelius is a grubby little daydreamer. Worse follows. He is a rock musician, or hopes to be one, but his taste isn't really very secure, he's not much on the guitar, and when he finally gets the chance to perform in public (at an amateur gig under an elevated highway) he's too spaced out to make any sense at all. It's the real world, in which time passes, taking us down. For Jerry, as the years pass, life seems to be a series of bad auditions. Most of his fellow denizens of Ladbroke Grove are in no better shape than he is; the Edwardian tapestry of lords and ladies (with two exceptions) turn out to be a klatch of petty entrepreneurs; Auchinek is a music agent, for instance, while Frank sells fake antiques to tourists at the Portobello Road market. Gradually Jerry achieves some success, on the stage, acting Harlequin; he has teamed up with his sister and Una Persson (she remains vital) and they all have sex together; playing games with themselves. His mother is also unchanged, or so it seems. She remains all appetite, she remains indomitable; because she survives the Cornelius clan survives. Then, in the last pages of the novel, she dies. Her death is not like the play-deaths earlier in the tetralogy. She is dead. She is dead. As the novel closes—for she is dead—Jerry is on his way to tell his pregnant sister the terrible news of the real fact of death.

There is no enclave secure against time. No style has a permanent lock on the shape of the world. No tune can last, certainly not as played on Jerry's dismal guitar. If you ask whether or not it is possible to maintain homeostasis in a decaying world, the answer is that all art constantly aspires towards the condition of Muzak. Entropy rots your heart out. There is a lot of ageing going on.

But that's not the final point of the novel, for Jerry Cornelius has, after all, survived the lacerating light-shows of our portion of the century, and in the intensest of venues; and at times his Pierrot heart fills with love that transcends his sustaining self-pity. From his scummy little balcony, he speaks to us at these times. SF, which is the least urban of genres, likes to tell us how to live in the Wild West, in case the need arises, and loves to show us how to hate Utopian city-states constructed by Utopian city-haters who live in suburbs behind hedges. In the Jerry Cornelius tetralogy Michael Moorcock has tried to tell us how to stay alive in the places where so many of us truly live. He has tried to tell us how to live here, in the deep cities of this world, in the years of their dying.

John Clute
London, February 1977

NOTE TO THE READER

Although these books may be read in any order, the reader might wish to know that the structure of the last volume reflects the structure of the overall tetralogy.

PRELIMINARY DATA

In Cambodia, a country lying between Vietnam and Thailand on the map, between n and zero on the time chart, is the magic city of Angkor, where once the great Khmer race lived. In the nineteenth century a French explorer rediscovered it in the jungle. It was subsequently resurrected by French archaeologists. The simple-living inhabitants, descendants of the Khmers, had two theories about the city—that it had been built by a race of giants and that the city had created itself when the world was created. Writing about Angkor in the *Sunday Times* (10/1/65) Maurice Wiggin said: "Did the citizens of Angkor have the future they wanted? Hardly. Yet they seemed adaptable, switching pragmatically from Hinduism to Buddhism, building to last. ('The most impressive ruins in the world.') But the great kings of Khmer are dust."

Built not merely to last but to exist for its age, towering over the huge statues and ziggurats of Angkor, stands the Angkor Hilton. According to the simple-living descendants of the Khmers, it is the chief evidence for the second theory.

On the roof of the Angkor Hilton is a glass conservatory or observatory, not unlike a miniature version of the old Crystal Palace. The building is the particular property of one of the hotel's regular customers. It contains a bed, a metal locker, a large astronomical telescope, and a marine chronometer dating from the eighteenth century. The chronometer is beautifully made, of steel and brass, and is probably one of the original clocks constructed in 1760 by John Harrison, the first man to make a really accurate marine chronometer. It stands on top of the locker, and below it, hanging from the handle, is a calendar. The year is 196–.

The owner of this equipment, Jerry Cornelius, was not in the observatory at that moment. He was wandering the grassy paths that wound among grey and brown statues or below the leafy branches of big trees where monkeys peered down at him and chattered. Cornelius was dressed incongruously for the place and climate, and even in the West his clothes would have had a slightly old-fashioned look about them; the high-heeled elastic-sided boots, for instance, were not at all in style, nor had they been for several years.

Cornelius was on his way to keep a date.

Serene and carved in ancient rock, the faces of Buddhas and the three aspects of Ishwara looked from terraces and archways; huge statues, bas-reliefs—probably the greatest clutter of deities and devils ever assembled in one place. Beneath an extravagantly bloated representation of Vishnu the Destroyer, one of Ishwara's three aspects, a tiny transistor radio played. It was Cornelius's radio. The tune was "Zoot's Suite" by Zoot Money's Big Roll Band.

Beside the radio, in the green-gold early-afternoon sunshine, a man sat at leisure while mosquitoes buzzed and chattering gibbons leaped from one half-reconstructed terrace to another. A Buddhist priest passed by, shaven and saffroned, and a group of brown children played among the massive statues of forgotten heroes. It was a pleasant afternoon, with a slight breeze fanning the jungle. A good time for idle speculation, thought Cornelius, sitting down beside the man and shaking hands.

They sat in the fallen stone palm of some minor Hindu divinity and took up the conversation where they had left off earlier.

Jerry Cornelius was a young man, with long, fine black hair that flowed to below his shoulders. He wore a black, double-breasted car coat and dark grey trousers. His tie was of black wool and his white shirt had a high collar. He was slim, with large dark eyes and large, long-fingered hands. The other man was an Indian, owlish and pudgy—perpetually smiling, no matter what he said—in shirtsleeves and cotton trousers.

Jeremiah Cornelius was a European of many parts; the Indian was a Brahmin physicist of some reputation, Professor Hira. They had met that morning while touring the city. It had been love at first sight.

The Brahmin physicist patted at the mosquitoes settling on his arms. "The Gnostics possessed a cosmology very similar, in many ways, to the Hindu and Buddhist. Interpretations varied, of course, but the figures were very close."

"What figures exactly?" Jerry asked politely.

"Well, for instance, the *mahāyuga*. Both Hindus and Gnostics give the figure as 4,320,000 years. That is an interesting coincidence from any point of view, eh?"

"What about the *kalpa*? I thought that was your word for a time cycle."

"Ah, no, that is a day or night of Brahma; 8,640 million years."

"As little as that?" said Jerry, without irony.

"The *mahāyuga* is divided into four *yugas*, or ages. The current cycle is nearing its end. The present age is the last of four."

"And what are they?"

"Oh, let me think… The *Satya Yuga*, the Golden Age. That accounted for the first four tenths of the cycle. Then we had the *Tretā Yuga*, the Second Age. That took care of another 1,296,000 years. The Third Age—the *Dvāpara Yuga*—can you hear the echoes of an ancient common language?—lasted for only two tenths of the whole cycle. I think that's right, don't you? How much we rely, these days, on our calculating machines. The *Kali Yuga*, of course, is the current age. It began, as I recall, on February eighteenth, 3102 BC."

"And what is the *Kali Yuga*?"

"The Dark Age, Mr Cornelius. Ha! Ha!"

"How long is that supposed to last?"

"Just one tenth of the *mahāyuga*."

"That gives us plenty of time."

"Oh, yes."

"Then at the end of the *manvantara* the cycle repeats itself, does it? The whole of history all over again!"

"Some believe so. Others think that the cycles vary slightly. It is basically an extension of our convictions concerning reincarnation. The strange thing is that modern physics begins to confirm these figures—in terms of the complete revolution of the galaxy and so on. I must admit that the more I read of the papers published these days, the more confused I become between what I was taught as a Hindu and what I have learned as a physicist. It requires increasing self-discipline to separate them in my mind."

"Why do you bother, professor?"

"My career, old man, at the University, would suffer if I let mysticism influence logic."

The Brahmin spoke slightly sardonically, and Jerry smiled. "Yet the cosmologies mingle and absorb one another," Jerry said. "There are people in Europe who believe that the *Vedas* describe a prehistoric civilisation as advanced, or more so, as our own. That would tie in with your first age, wouldn't it?"

"Some of my friends have wondered about that, too. It is possible, naturally, but not likely. Exquisite parables, Mr Cornelius, but nothing more. Not the mythical vestiges of a great science, I fear. The embroidered remnants of a great philosophy, perhaps."

"Pleasant embroidery."

"You are kind to think so. Perhaps I should not say so, but it occasionally crosses my mind to wonder why, in all the mystic cosmologies, even in some of the modern so-called parasciences, our own age is always described as the age of chaos and contention. A comment, my logical side argues, on why people turn to mysticism. The past age was always better."

"Childhood is the happiest time of life except when you're a child," said Jerry.

"I understand you. True."

"Whereas your philosophers produced beautiful metaphors that were not 'true', maybe?"

"You are pushing me too far; but you have studied the *Vedas*? It seems that more Westerners study Sanskrit than we. And we read Einstein."

"So do we."

"You have more time for everything over there, old man. You are at the end of your *manvantara*, eh? We have begun a new one."

"I wonder."

"I do not speak seriously—as a Hindu—but there are shorter cycles within the ages. Several of my more metaphysically inclined acquaintances have predicted that we are at the end of such a cycle."

"But our affairs diminish in significance compared with a span of even 432,000 years."

"That's a Western idea, Mr Cornelius." Hira smiled. "What is Time? How long is a millisecond or a millennium? If the old Hindus were right, then we have met in Angkor before and shall again—and the date will always be today's, October thirty-first, 196–. Will anything have changed, I wonder, in the next *manvantara*? Will gods walk the earth? Will man be—?"

Jerry Cornelius got up. "Who knows? Let's compare notes then. I'll be seeing you, professor."

"This time next *manvantara*?"

"If you like."

"Where are you off to now?" The Indian also rose, handing Jerry the little radio.

"Thanks. I'm going to Phnôm Penh Airport and then to London. I want to order a guitar. And see my mum."

Hira followed him through the ruins, climbing over slabs of stone. "You're at the Angkor Hilton, aren't you? Why not stay one more night at the hotel?"

"Well, all right."

That night they lay in bed together, talking and smoking. A heavy mosquito net had been drawn round the bed, but they could see through it, and through the glass beyond, to the still sky.

"It makes you wonder just how close we are to finding the great equation." Hira's voice hummed like an insect through the warm air. Jerry was trying to get to sleep. "The total equation. The final equation. The ultimate equation, drawing all the information together. Will we ever?"

"The climate seems right," said Jerry sleepily.

"In your terms it is time for a new messiah—a messiah of the Age of Science. I suppose that is blasphemy. Has the genius been born yet? Will we recognise him when he comes?"

"That's what they all wonder, don't they?"

"Ah, Mr Cornelius, what a bewildering, topsy-turvy world this is."

Jerry turned over to his side, his back to the professor. "I'm not so sure," he said. "The world seems to be steering a fairly straight course at last."

"But to where?"

"That, professor, is the snag."

"She was talking about the final equation, this woman I met in Delhi last year. A passing affair, you know, and I'm glad it was. She gave me some very interesting food for speculation, this Miss Brunner, old man. She seemed to know…"

"Bully for her."

"Bully? Yes…"

Jerry Cornelius fell asleep.

PHASE

I

It was raining.

The house was in south-east London, in Blackheath. It stood back from the main road, looming out of its overgrown garden. The gravel drive was weedy, and the house needed painting. It had originally been painted a light mauve. Through the grimy ground-floor windows Jerry Cornelius could glimpse five people seated in a big front room, full of dark furniture and poorly lit. The fire gave more light than the standard lamp in one corner. The faces were all shadowed. On the mantelpiece stood a baroque figurine of Diana holding two candlesticks; there were two candles in each stick.

The garage door slammed, and Jerry made no effort to become any less visible, but the bulky tweed-coated man didn't notice him as he patted water from his heavy black beard, took off his hat, and opened the door. He wiped his feet and went inside. Jerry had recognised him as Mr Smiles. Mr Smiles owned the house.

After a moment Jerry went up to the door and took out his key ring. He found the right key and opened the door. He saw Mr Smiles enter the front room.

The hallway smelled a little damp, in spite of the radiator burning close to the hat rack; and the walls, each painted a different colour (tangerine, red, black, and blue), were all cold as Jerry leaned on first one and then another.

Jerry was dressed in his usual black car coat, dark trousers and high heels. His hair was wet.

He folded his arms and settled down to wait.

"What's the time? My watch has stopped." Mr Smiles entered the room, shaking rain off his Robin Hood hat and still patting at his beard. He walked to the fire and stood there, turning the hat round and round to dry it.

The five others said nothing. All seemed introspective, hardly aware of his arrival. Then one of them got up and approached Mr Smiles. His name was Mr Lucas. He had the decadent good looks of a Roman patrician. He was forty-five and a successful casino owner. Except for Mr Smiles (who was forty-nine), he was the oldest.

"Twelve-forty, Mr Smiles. He's late."

Mr Smiles concentrated on drying his hat. "I've never known him not to do something he said he'd do, if that's any comfort," he said.

"Oh, it is," said Miss Brunner.

Miss Brunner was sitting nearest to the fire. She was a sharp-faced, attractive young woman with the look of a predator. She sprawled back in her chair with her legs crossed. One foot tapped at the air.

Mr Smiles turned towards her.

"He'll come, Miss Brunner." He gave her a glare. "He'll come." His tone was self-assuring.

Mr Lucas glanced at his watch again.

Miss Brunner's foot tapped more quickly. "Why are you so certain, Mr Smiles?"

"I know him—at least, as well as anyone could. He's reliable, Miss Brunner."

Miss Brunner was a computer programmer of some experience and power. Seated closest to her was Dimitri, her slave, lover, and sometime unwilling pimp. She wore a straight fawn Courrèges suit and matching buttoned boots. He also wore a Courrèges suit of dark blue-and-brown tweed. Her hair was red and long, curving outward at the ends. It was nice hair, but not on her. He was the son of Dimitri Koutrouboussis, rich, with the fresh, ingenuous appearance of a boy. His disguise was complete.

Behind Miss Brunner and Dimitri, in shadow, sat Mr Crookshank, the entertainers' agent. Mr Crookshank was very fat and tall. He had a heavy gold signet ring on the third finger of his right hand. It gave him the common touch. He wore a silk Ivy League suit.

In the corner, opposite Mr Crookshank, nearer the fire, sat dark Mr Powys, hunched in his perpetual neurotic stoop. Mr Powys, who lived comfortably off the inheritance left him by his mine-owning great-uncle, sipped a glass of Bell's cream whisky, staring at it as he sipped.

The fire did not heat the room sufficiently. Even Mr

Smiles, who was usually unaffected by cold, rubbed his hands together after he had taken off his coat. Mr Smiles was a banker, main owner of the Smiles Bank, which had catered to the linen trade since 1832. The bank was not doing well, though Mr Smiles couldn't complain personally. Mr Smiles poured himself a large glass of Teacher's whisky and moved back to the fire.

None of them was well acquainted, except with Miss Brunner, who had introduced them all. They all knew Miss Brunner.

She uncrossed her legs and smoothed her skirt, smiling up unpleasantly at the bearded man. "It's unusual to find such confidence these days." She paused and looked round at the others. "I think…" She opened her handbag and began picking at its contents.

"What do you think?" Mr Smiles spoke sharply. "When I first put this deal to you, Miss Brunner, you were uncertain about it. Now you're impatient to get started. What do you think, then, Miss Brunner?"

"I think we shouldn't include him in our plans. Let's get going now, while he's not expecting anything. He could be planning some kind of double-cross. We stand to lose too much by hanging about waiting for Cornelius. I don't trust him, Mr Smiles."

"You don't trust him because you haven't met him and given him the Brunner Test, is that it?" Mr Lucas kicked at a log sticking from the fire. "We couldn't get into that house without Cornelius's knowledge of those booby traps of his father's. If Cornelius doesn't come, then we'll have to give up the whole idea."

Miss Brunner's sharp teeth showed as she smiled again. "You're getting old and cautious, Mr Lucas. And Mr Smiles, by the sound of it, is getting soft as well. As far as I'm concerned, the risk is part of it."

"You silly cow!" Dimitri was often rude to Miss Brunner in public, much as he loved to fear her. Public insults; private punishments. "We're not all in it for the risks; we're in it for what old Cornelius hid in his house. Without Jerry Cornelius, we'll never get it. We need him. That's the truth."

"I'm pleased to hear it." Jerry's voice was sardonic. He entered the room rather theatrically and closed the door behind him.

Miss Brunner looked him over. He was very tall, and the pale face, framed by the hair, resembled the young Swinburne's. His black eyes did not seem at all kindly. He was about twenty-seven and had been, so they said, a Jesuit. He had something of a Church intellectual's decadent, ascetic appearance. He had possibilities, she thought.

Jerry dropped his head a trifle as he turned and gave Miss Brunner a slightly amused stare, half-chiding. She crossed her legs and began tapping. He walked gracefully towards Mr Smiles and with a certain degree of pleasure shook hands.

Mr Smiles sighed. "I'm glad you could make it, Mr Cornelius. How soon can we start?"

Jerry shrugged. "As soon as you like. I need a day or so to do a few things."

"Tomorrow?" Miss Brunner's voice was pitched

somewhat higher than usual.

"In three days." Cornelius pursed his lips. "Sunday."

Mr Powys spoke from behind his glass. "Three days is too much. The longer we wait, the more chance there is of someone getting to know what we're planning. Don't forget that Simons and Harvey both backed out, and Harvey in particular isn't well known for his tact and diplomacy."

"Don't worry about them," Cornelius said with finality.

"What have you done?" Miss Brunner's voice was still sharp.

"Nothing much. They're taking a cruise on a tramp bound for Odessa. It'll be a long trip, and they won't mix with the crew."

"How did you get them to go?" Mr Lucas dropped his eyes as Cornelius turned.

"Well," said Jerry, "there were one or two things they wanted. On condition that they took the trip, I fixed them up."

"What things?" asked Mr Crookshank with interest. Jerry ignored him.

"What have you to do that's so important?" Miss Brunner enquired.

"I want to visit the house before our trip."

"Why?"

"For my own reasons, Miss Brunner."

Mr Powys's brooding Welsh face didn't look up. "I'd like to know just why you're helping us, mind you, Mr Cornelius."

"Would you understand if I told you that it was for revenge?"

"Revenge." Mr Powys shook his head rapidly. "Oh, yes. We all get these grudges from time to time, don't we?"

"Then it's revenge," Jerry said lightly. "Now, Mr Smiles has told you my conditions, I think. You must burn the house to the ground when you've got what you wanted, and you must leave my brother Francis and my sister Catherine unharmed. There is also an old servant, John. He must not be hurt in any way."

"The rest of the staff?" Dimitri waved an impolite and questioning hand.

"Do whatever you like. You'll be taking on some help, I understand?"

"About twenty men. Mr Smiles has arranged them. He says they'll be sufficient." Mr Lucas glanced at Mr Smiles, who nodded.

"They should be," Jerry said thoughtfully. "The house is well guarded, but naturally they won't call the police. With our special equipment you ought to be all right. Don't forget to burn the house."

"Mr Smiles has already reminded us of that, Mr Cornelius," said Dimitri. "We will do exactly as you say."

Jerry turned up the wide collar of his coat. "Right. I'll be off."

"Take care, Mr Cornelius," Miss Brunner said smoothly as he went out.

"Oh, I will, I think," he said.

The six people did not talk much after Cornelius

had left. Only Miss Brunner moved to another chair. She seemed out of sorts.

"What do we know," she said, "about his *mother*?"

2

Music filled the old Duesenberg as Jerry Cornelius drove towards the Kent coast—Zoot Money, The Who, The Beatles. Jerry played only the best.

The volume was turned up to full blast. There were four speakers in the car, and it was impossible for Jerry to hear the sound of the engine. In the spring clip near the steering wheel the contents of a glass danced to the thud of the bass. From time to time Cornelius would reach for the glass, take a sip, and fix it back in the clip. Once he put his hand inside the glove compartment and brought it out full of pills. He had not slept for the best part of a week, and the pills no longer stopped him from feeling edgy; but he crammed his mouth with them, just the same, washing them down. A little later he took out a half-bottle of Bell's and refilled the glass.

The road ahead was wet, and rain still beat at the windscreen. The two pairs of wipers swished away in time with the music. Though the heater was on, he felt cold.

Just outside Dover he stopped at a filling station while he rolled himself a thin cigarette out of liquorice paper and Old Holborn. He paid the man, lit his cigarette, and rode on in the general direction of the coast, turning off onto a side road and eventually driving down the main street of the harbour village of Southquay, strains of guitars, organs and high voices drifting in the car's wake. The sea was black under the overcast sky. He drove slowly along the quayside, the car's wheels bumping on cobbles. He switched off the tape.

There was a small hotel set back from the road. It was called The Yachtsman. Its sign showed a smiling man in yachting gear. Behind him was a view of the harbour as seen from the hotel. The sign moved a little in the wind. Jerry backed the Duesenberg into the hotel's courtyard, left the keys in the ignition, and got out. He put his hands in the high pockets of his coat and stood stretching his legs by the car for a moment, looking over the black water at the moored boats. One of them was his launch, which he'd had converted from a modern lifeboat.

He glanced back at the hotel, noting that no lights had gone on and that no-one seemed to be stirring. He crossed to the waterside. A metal ladder led down into the sea. He climbed down a few rungs and then jumped from the ladder to the deck of his launch. Pausing for a moment to get his sea legs, he made straight for the well-kept bridge. He didn't switch on the lights, but by finding the instruments by touch got the motor warming up.

He went out on deck again and cast off.

Soon he was steering his way out of the harbour towards the open sea.

Only the man in the harbourmaster's office saw him leave. Happily for Jerry, the man was quite as corrupt as the six people who had been at the house in Blackheath. He had, as they used to say, his price.

Steering a familiar course, Jerry headed the boat towards the coast of Normandy, where his late father had built his fake Le Corbusier château. It was an ancient building, built well before the Second World War.

Once outside the three-mile limit, Jerry switched on the radio and got the latest station, Radio K-Nine ("The Station With Bite"). There was some funny stuff on; it sounded like a mixture of Greek and Persian music very badly played. It was probably by one of the new groups the publicity people were still trying in vain to push. They were completely non-musical themselves, so still found it a mystery that one group should be popular and another unpopular, were convinced that a new sound would start things moving for them again. All that was over—for the time being at least, thought Jerry. He changed stations until he got a reasonable one.

The music echoed over the water. Although he was careful not to show any lights, Jerry could be heard half a mile away; but when he saw the faint outline of the coast ahead, he switched off the radio.

After a while his father's fake Le Corbusier château came in sight, a large six-storey building with that quaint, dated appearance that all the 'futuristic' buildings of the twenties and thirties had. To boot, this château had a dash of German expressionism in its architecture.

For Jerry the house symbolised the very spirit of transience, and he enjoyed the feeling he got from looking at its silhouette, much as he sometimes enjoyed listening to last year's hits. The house stood on the very edge of a cliff that curved steeply above the nearest village, some four miles distant. A searchlight was trained on the house, making it look rather like some grotesque war memorial. Jerry knew the house was staffed by a small private army of German mercenaries, men who were as much part of the past as the house and yet intratemporally reflected something of the spirit of the 1970s.

It was November 196–, however, as Jerry cut the engine and drifted on the current he knew would carry him towards the cliff beneath the house.

The cliff was worse than sheer. It sloped outward about a hundred feet up and was loaded with alarm devices. Not even Wolfe could have taken it. The nature of the cliff was to Jerry Cornelius an advantage, for it hid his boat from the TV scanners in the house. The radar did not sweep low enough to find his launch, but the TV cameras were trained on any likely place where someone might attempt a landing. Jerry's brother Frank did not know of the secret entrance.

He moored the boat to the cliff by means of the powerful suction cups he had brought for the purpose.

The cups had metal rings in them, and Jerry tied his mooring lines to the rings. He would be away again before the tide went out.

Part of the cliff was made of plastic. Cornelius tapped lightly on it, waiting a couple of moments as it inched inward and a gaunt, anxious face peered out at him. It was the face of a lugubrious Scot, Jerry's old servant and mentor, John Gnatbeelson.

"Ah, sir!"

The face retreated, leaving the entrance clear.

"Is she all right, John?" Jerry asked as he eased himself into the metal-walled cubicle behind the plastic door. John Gnatbeelson stepped backward and then forward to close the door. He was about six feet four, a gangling man with almost non-existent cheekbones and a wisp of chin whiskers. He wore an old Norfolk jacket and corduroy trousers. His bones seemed barely joined together, and he moved loosely like a badly controlled puppet.

"She's not dead, sir, I think," Gnatbeelson assured Jerry. "It's fine to see you, sir. I hope you've returned for good this time, sir, to kick Mr Frank out of our house." He glared into the middle distance. "He had… had…" The old man's eyes filled with tears.

"Cheer up, John. What's he been doing now?"

"That's what I don't know, sir. I haven't been allowed to see Miss Catherine for the past week. *He* says she's sleeping. Sleeping. What kind of sleep lasts for a week, sir?"

"Could be a number of kinds." Jerry spoke calmly enough. "Drugs, I expect."

"God knows he uses enough of them himself, sir. He lives on them. All he ever eats is bars of chocolate."

"Catherine wouldn't use sleepers voluntarily, I shouldn't think."

"She never would, sir."

"Is she still in her old rooms?"

"Yes, sir. But there's a guard on the door."

"Have you prepared for that?"

"I have, but I am worried."

"Of course you are. And you've switched off the master control for this entrance?"

"It seemed unnecessary, sir, but I have done it."

"Better safe than sorry, John."

"I suppose so, aye. But there again, it would only be a matter of time before…"

"It's all a matter of time, John. Let's get going. If the control's dead, we won't be able to use the lift."

"No, sir. We must climb."

"Off we go, then."

They left the metal chamber and entered a similar, slightly larger one. John lit the way with his torch. A lift cage became visible, the shaft rising above it. Paralleling the cables and running up one side into the darkness was a metal ladder. John tucked the torch into the waistband of his trousers and stepped back. Jerry reached the ladder and began to climb.

They went up in silence for more than fifty feet until they stood at the top of the shaft. Ahead of them were five entrances to corridors. They took the central entrance.

The corridor twisted and turned for a long time. It formed part of a complicated maze and, even though the two men were familiar with it, they sometimes hesitated at various turnings and forks.

Eventually, and with some relief, they entered a white, neon-lighted room, which housed a small control console. The Scotsman went to the panel and clicked a switch. A red light above the panel went off and a green one went on. Dials quivered, and several monitor screens focused on various parts of the route they had just taken. Views of the room at the bottom of the shaft, the shaft itself, the corridors in the maze—now brilliantly lit— came and went on the screens. The equipment operated in silence.

On the door leading out of the room was a fairly large ovoid of a milky greenish colour. John pressed his palm against it. Responding to the palm print, which it recognised, the door slid open. They entered a short tunnel, which led them to an identical door. This John opened in the same way.

Now they stood in a dark library. Through a transparent wall to their right they could see the sea, like black marble streaked with veins of grey and white.

Most of the other three walls were covered with shelves of pink fibreglass. They were filled mainly with paperbacks. The half-dozen or so books bound in leather and titled in gold stood out incongruously. John shone his light on them and smiled at Jerry, who was embarrassed.

"They're still there, sir. He doesn't often come here;

otherwise he might have got rid of them. Not that it would matter that much, for I have another set."

Jerry winced and looked at the books. One of the titles was *Time Search Through the Declining West* by Jeremiah Cornelius, MAHS; another was called *Toward the Ultimate Paradox*, and beside it was *The Ethical Simulation*. Jerry felt he was right to be embarrassed.

Part of the library wall, naturally enough, was false. It swung back to show a white metal door and a button. Jerry pressed the button and the door opened.

Another lift cage.

John stooped and picked up a small case before they got in and went up. It was one of the few lifts in the house that, as far as they knew, did not register on one of the many control panels located in the château.

On the sixth floor the lift stopped, and John opened the door and looked cautiously out. The landing was empty. They both left the lift, and the door (a wall-length painting reminiscent of Picasso at his latest and tritest) slid back into place.

The room they wanted was in a passage off the main landing. They walked silently to the corner, glanced round, and ducked back again.

They had seen the guard. He had an automatic rifle crooked in his arm. He was a big, fat German with the appearance of a eunuch. He had looked very wakeful—hoping, perhaps, for an opportunity to use his Belgian gun.

Now John opened the case he'd been carrying. He took out a small steel crossbow, very modern and beautifully made, and handed it to Jerry Cornelius. Jerry held it in one hand, waiting for the moment when the guard would look completely away from him. Shortly, the man's attention shifted towards the window at the end of the passage.

Jerry stepped out, aimed the crossbow, and pulled the trigger. But the guard had heard him and jumped. The bolt grazed his neck. There was only one bolt.

As the guard began to bring up his gun, Jerry ran towards him and grabbed the fingers of his right hand, hauling them off the gun. One finger snapped. The guard gurgled and his mouth gaped, showing that he was tongueless. He kicked at Jerry as John came in with a knife, missed his neck, and stabbed him through the left eye. The blade went in for almost its entire six inches, driving downward and coming out just below the left ear. As the German's CNS packed it in, his body was momentarily paralysed.

It softened as Jerry lowered it to the floor; he reached down and slid the knife out of the German's face, handing it to John who was as limp as the corpse.

"Get away from here, John," Jerry muttered. "If I make it, I'll see you in the cliff room."

As John Gnatbeelson rolled off, Jerry turned the handle of the door. It was of the conventional kind, and the key was in the lock. He turned the key when the door resisted. The door opened. Jerry took the key out of the lock. Inside the room he closed the door quietly and locked it again.

He stood in a woman's bedroom.

The heavy curtains were drawn across the big

windows. The place smelled of stale air and misery. He crossed the familiar room and found the bedside lamp, switching it on.

Red light filled the place. A beautiful girl lay in a pale dress on the bed. Her features were delicate and resembled his own. Her black hair was tangled. Her small breasts rose and fell jerkily, and her breathing was shallow. She was not sleeping at all naturally. Jerry looked for hypodermic marks and found them in her upper right arm. Plainly she hadn't used a needle on herself. Frank had done that.

Jerry stroked her bared shoulder. "Catherine." He bent down and kissed her cold, soft lips, caressing her. Anger, self-pity, despair, passion were all there then, flooding up to the surface, and for once he didn't stop them. "Catherine."

She didn't move. Jerry was crying now. His body trembled. He tried to control the trembling and failed. He gripped her hand, and it was like holding hands with a corpse. He tightened his grip, as if hoping pain would wake her. Then he dropped it and stood up.

"The shit!"

He pulled the curtains back from the windows and opened them. The night air blew away the odour in the room.

On her dressing table there were no cosmetics, only bottles of drugs and several hypodermics.

The labels on the bottles were in Frank's tiny printing. Frank had been experimenting.

Outside, someone shouted and began to bang on the metal door. He stared at it uncomprehendingly for a moment, then crossed to it and shot bolts at top and bottom.

A sharper, colder voice interrupted the yelling.

"What's the trouble? Has someone been boorish enough to enter Miss Catherine's room without her permission?"

It was Frank's voice, and Frank doubtless guessed that his brother Jerry was in the room.

There were confused shouts from the guards, and Frank had to raise his voice. "Whoever you are, you'll suffer for invading my sister's privacy. You can't get out. If she's harmed or disturbed in any way, you won't die for a long time, I promise. But you'll wish you could."

"As corny as ever, Frank!" Jerry shouted back. "I know you know it's me—and I know you're shit-scared. I've more right here than you. I own this house!"

"Then you should have stayed and not turned it over to me and Catherine. I meant what I said, Jerry!"

"Send your krauts off and come in and talk it over. All I want is Catherine."

"I'm not that naïve. You'll never know what I fed her, Jerry. Only I can wake her up. It's like magic, isn't it? She's well turned on. If I turned her off now, you wouldn't be so keen on hopping into bed with her after ten minutes." Frank laughed. "You'd need a dose of what I've got out here before you'd feel up to it—and then you wouldn't want it any more. You can't have your fix and make it, Jerry!"

Frank was in high spirits. Jerry wondered what his brother had found to pep him up. Frank was always after a new synthesis and, as a good chemist, usually came up with a nice new habit every so often. Was it the same stuff as Catherine had in her veins right now? Probably not.

"Throw in your needle and come in with your veins clear, Frank." Jerry joined in the spirit of the thing. He took something out of his pocket and waited, but Frank didn't seem willing to rise to this. Bullets began to rattle on the door. They'd soon stop as the ricochets got too much for Frank. They stopped.

Jerry went to the bed and heaved his sister off it. Then he put her down again. It was no good. He wouldn't have a chance of getting out with her. He'd have to leave her and hope that Frank's mind didn't turn to thoughts of murder. It was unlikely. Slow death was the only worthwhile kind in Frank's book.

From the inside pocket of his coat Jerry brought out a flat box like a snuff box. He opened it. There were two small filters there. He packed one into each nostril and clamped his mouth shut, sealing it with some surgical tape from another pocket.

Then he unbolted the door and slowly turned the key. He opened the door slightly. Frank stood some distance away, talking to four of his storm troopers. Frank's skin was grey, drawn over his near-fleshless skeleton like a lifeless film of plastic. They hadn't yet noticed that the door was open.

Jerry tossed the grenade into the passage. They saw it fall. Only Frank recognised the nerve grenade for what it was, and he dashed off down the passage without stopping to give the guards the benefit of his knowledge.

Jerry stepped swiftly out of the room and closed the door tight behind him. The guards tried to aim at him, but the gas was already working. As they jerked like epileptics and fell down to bounce about spasmodically on the floor, Jerry gave them an amused, appreciative glance.

Jerry Cornelius went after Frank Cornelius. Frank pushed the button of the lift that went down to the library. When Frank saw Jerry, he swore and ran towards the end of the passage and the stairs. Jerry decided that he didn't want Frank alive any more, and he drew out his pistol. The air pistol could hold a magazine of a hundred silver needles and was just as effective at short range as any small-calibre pistol—and far more accurate. Neither was it messy. Its only drawback was that it had to be repressured after every volley.

Jerry ran after his brother. Frank was evidently unarmed. He was scuttling down the spiral stairs now. Leaning on the banister, Jerry took aim at Frank's head.

But when he put his arm down, he realised that he'd caught a sniff of the nerve gas himself, for the arm jumped twice and he involuntarily pulled the trigger. The needles went wide, and Frank had left the stairs on the third floor. He was now out of sight.

Jerry heard voices and noisy feet and knew that Frank had called in another section of the militia. He had no more nerve bombs with him. It was time, perhaps, to be leaving.

He ran back down the landing. The lift was waiting for him. Frank might assume that it wasn't working, since he'd had no luck himself. He got into the lift and went down to the library. It was empty. In the library he paused and hauled his books off the shelf. He opened the door in the window and stepped out onto the balcony. Then he flung the books into the sea, re-entered the library, closed the door carefully, and knocked on the other entrance. It slid back. John was here. He still looked pale.

"What happened, sir?"

"Maybe he'll never guess completely, John, so you might get away with it. He's fazed, I think. Now it's up to you. On Sunday you must somehow get Catherine away from the house and into the lodge on the village side of the grounds. There'll probably be enough confusion and you'll be able to do it easily. Don't make a mistake. I want you both at that lodge. And Sunday starts at about 10 p.m., I'd guess."

"Yes, sir—but…"

"No time for details, John. Do it. Don't bother to see me out."

Jerry Cornelius went through the control room, and John shut off the equipment again.

Then Jerry was on his way, torch in hand, back to his boat.

Within twenty minutes he was looking up at the house as his launch throbbed towards the English coast. The house was full of light now. It looked as if the residents were having a party.

It was still an hour until dawn. He had a chance of making it back to Southquay before the new man came on watch at the harbourmaster's office.

3

On Sunday morning Miss Brunner and Dimitri left for Blackheath. She locked the door of her Holland Park house and tucked the note for the milkman into an empty bottle on the step. Dimitri had the Lotus 15 ready and running by the time she had put on her gloves and walked daintily down the path.

Later, as they waited for the Knightsbridge traffic to move, Miss Brunner decided that she would drive, and she and Dimitri changed places. They were used to changing places; it held them together in these uncertain times.

"Mr Cornelius had better be there," Miss Brunner said obsessively as she drove down Sloane Street, which was less crowded than it would have been on a weekday.

Dimitri sat back and smoked. He'd had a tiring night, and he hadn't enjoyed himself as much as usual, particularly since Miss Brunner had insisted on calling him Cornelius the whole time.

Let her work it out, he thought. He was rather jealous of Cornelius, all the same; it had taken him two cups of strong coffee when he'd got up to convince himself that he was not in any way Jerry Cornelius. Miss Brunner, on the other hand, had evidently not been so easily convinced, and she was as bad today as she'd been since Thursday.

Well, with luck it would all be over by Monday, and they could begin the next phase of their plan—a much more sophisticated phase that involved thought and little energetic action.

It was a pity that attacking the house was the only way. He hadn't liked the idea at all when it was first proposed, but since he'd had time to think about it, he was half looking forward to it. The fact disturbed him.

Miss Brunner drove the throbbing Lotus 15 over Westminster Bridge with gusto, entered the maze of streets beyond, then went down Old Kent Road.

She had decided that she must have Jerry Cornelius, but she knew that this was one situation in which she must act for herself and not rely on Dimitri. A savoury chick, she thought, a nice spicy chick. She began to feel better.

Mr Crookshank, the entertainers' agent, kissed Little Miss Dazzle goodbye. Little Miss Dazzle was quite naked and did not appear on stage like that, if for no other reason than that the public would see that she was in fact equipped with the daintiest masculine genitals.

It was not yet time, Mr Crookshank had decided, to

reveal that particular secret; not while Miss Dazzle was still smoothing up to the number one spot in the Top Ten Girl Chart within three days to a week with every disc she cut. When number five came to be her ceiling, then a few rumours might start. Then perhaps a marriage, he thought, though he'd hate to lose her.

Mr Crookshank's Rolls, complete with chauffeur, waited downstairs outside the entrance hall to Miss Dazzle's Bloomsbury flat.

The chauffeur knew the way.

Mr Crookshank lit a panatella as the car cruised off in the general direction of Blackfriars Bridge. He switched on the radio and, as luck would have it, Little Miss Dazzle's latest hit on Big Beat Call, the non-stop pop programme, was playing. It was a moving song, and Mr Crookshank was duly moved. The words seemed to be for him.

> *I am a part of you, the heart of you,*
> *I want to start with you,*
> *And know…*

The beat changed from 4/4 to 3/4, and the guitars tumbled into the fifth when she sang:

> *Just what it is,*
> *Just what it is,*
> *Just what it is,*
> *I want to know.*

He looked out of the window as the car went down Farringdon Street towards the bridge. The Sunday workers all seemed to be moving in the same direction, as if the voice of the lemming had been heard in the land. In a philosophical mood, Mr Crookshank decided that it had been heard indeed, through the whole of Europe.

Mr Powys was running late, for Sunday was normally his day of rest, and he had got up early only after he had realised that he was due in Blackheath that morning. He left his Hyde Park Gate maisonette with a shaving cut on his face and yesterday's shirt on his back. He got his blue Aston Martin from the garage round the corner and put the top down so that the wet breeze would wake him up as he drove.

He switched on the radio for the same purpose, though he was too late to hear Little Miss Dazzle's 'Just What It Is'. Instead he came in on the middle of Tall Tom's Tailmen singing 'Suckers Deserve It'. If Mr Powys had a destiny, then Tall Tom's Tailmen were singing its tune—not that it occurred to Mr Powys, but then he was like that. The only thing the song did for him at that moment was to make him feel hungry, though he didn't know why. His thoughts turned to Miss Brunner and Dimitri, both of whom he knew intimately. In fact, it was extremely unlikely that he would have agreed to this venture if he hadn't known them so well.

Miss Brunner and Dimitri had a persuasive manner.

Except in moments of extreme sobriety, they were usually mingled together in his mind, Miss Brunner and Dimitri.

Mr Powys was a baffled, unhappy man.

He drove through the park under the impression that the air was clearer there, turned left and entered Knightsbridge, London's fabulous thieves' quarter, where every shop doorway (or, to be more accurate, every shop) held a thief of some description. Sloane Street was also his choice, but he went over Battersea Bridge and realised only after he'd reached Clapham Common that he'd made a mistake and was going to be later than ever.

By the time all the cars had crossed the river, Mr Smiles was having breakfast in his Blackheath house and wondering how he'd got into this in the first place. His knowledge of the information (probably on microfilm) to be found in old Cornelius's house had come from a friend of Frank Cornelius, a successful drug importer who supplied Frank with the rarer chemicals for his experiments. In a high moment Frank had let something slip, and Mr Harvey, the importer, had later let the same thing slip to Mr Smiles, also in a high moment.

Only Mr Smiles had fully realised the significance of the information, if it was correct, for he knew the City better than it knew him. He had told Miss Brunner, and Miss Brunner had organised it from there.

Mr Smiles had then got in touch with Jerry Cornelius, whom he hadn't seen for some time—not, in fact, since the day he and Jerry had robbed the City United Bank of some two million pounds and, with a million each, split up. The investigation by the police had been very half-hearted, as if they were concentrating on the important crimes of the day, realising that the inflating pound was no longer worth attempting to protect.

Mr Smiles could read the signs, for he was something of a visionary. He could see that the entire Western European economy, including Sweden and Switzerland, was soon to collapse. The information Mr Harvey had kindly passed on to him would probably hasten the collapse, but it would, if used properly, put Mr Smiles and his colleagues on top. They would hold pretty well nearly all the power there was to hold when anarchy at last set in.

Mr Smiles toyed with a fried egg, wondering why the yolks always broke these days.

In his permanently booked room in The Yachtsman, Jerry Cornelius had woken up at seven o'clock that morning and dressed himself in a lemon shirt with small ebony cufflinks, a wide black cravat, dark green waistcoat and matching hipsters, black socks and black handmade boots. He had washed his fine hair, and now he brushed it carefully until it shone.

Then he brushed one of his double-breasted black car coats and put it on.

He pulled on black calf gloves and was ready to face the world as soon as he slipped on his dark glasses.

From the bed, he picked up what appeared to be a dark leather toilet case. He snapped it open to check that his needle gun was pressured. He put the gun back and closed the case.

Holding the case in his left hand, he went downstairs; nodded to the proprietor, who nodded back; and got into the newly polished Duesenberg.

He sat in the car for a moment, looking out over the grey sea.

There was still a quarter of a glass of Bell's in the clip on the dashboard. He took it out, wound down the window, and threw the glass to the ground. He reached into the glove compartment and found a wrapped, fresh glass, fixed it in the clip and half-filled it from his bottle. Then he started the engine, turned the car around, and drove off, switching on the tape as soon as he was on Southquay's main street.

John, George, Paul and Ringo serenaded him with the old standard 'Baby's in Black'.

"Oh dear what can I do, baby's in black and I'm feeling blue…"

They were still his favourites.

"She thinks of him and so she dresses in black, and though he'll never come back, she's dressed in black."

Halfway to Blackheath he stopped off at a newsagent's shop and bought himself two Mars bars, two cups of strong black coffee, and two pounds of newsprint labelled NEWS SECTION, BUSINESS SECTION, LEISURE SECTION, ARTS SECTION, POP SECTION, CAR SECTION, COMIC SUPPLEMENT, COLOUR SUPPLEMENT, NOVEL SUPPLEMENT and HOLIDAY ADVERTISING SUPPLEMENT. The

News Section was a single sheet and the news was brief, to the point, uninterpreted. Jerry didn't read it. In fact, he didn't read anything except part of the Comic Supplement. There was plenty to look at. Jerry was well catered for.

He ate his sweets, drank his coffee, and folded up his sections and left them on the table, by way of a tip. Then he went back to his car to continue his journey to Blackheath.

He found that he didn't need to eat much, because he could live off other people's energy just as well. It was exhausting for them, of course. He didn't keep many acquaintances long, and Catherine was the only person off whom he hadn't fed. Indeed, it had been his delight to feed *her* with some of his stolen vitality. She hadn't liked it much, but she'd need it when he eventually got her away from that house and back to normal again, if he could ever get her back to normal.

He would certainly kill Frank when they raided the house. Frank's final needle would come from Jerry's gun. It would give him his final kick—the one he kept looking for.

Only Mr Lucas hadn't arrived by two o'clock, and they gave him up, feeling annoyed with him—which wasn't quite fair, for Mr Lucas had been stabbed to death in Islington the previous evening and robbed of the best part of his casino's takings by a much-embittered all-time loser who, by the following Monday, would fall downstairs and kill himself while taking the money to the bank.

Miss Brunner and Dimitri, Mr Smiles, Mr Crookshank

and Mr Powys were all looking at a map, which Mr Smiles had laid out on the table. Jerry Cornelius stood by the window smoking a thin cigarette and half-listening to them as they talked over the details of the expedition.

Mr Smiles pointed one of his strong fingers at a cross that had been drawn roughly in the middle of the English Channel between Dover and Normandy. "That's where the boat will be waiting. The men were all hired by me in Tangier. They answered an advertisement. At first they thought they were going to shoot Africans, but I managed to talk them round. They consist mainly of white South Africans, Belgians and French. There are a couple of British ex-officers. I put them in charge, of course. Apart from the South Africans, they got keener when I told them that they'd be fighting mainly Germans. Amazing how some people manage to hang on, isn't it?"

"Isn't it?" Mr Powys was, as ever, a trifle uncertain. "They'll be anchored here waiting for us, will they?"

"We thought that was best, you know. Actually, coastguard patrols aren't seen about as often as they were. We won't need to worry too much."

Miss Brunner pointed at the village near the Cornelius mansion. "What about this?"

"An advance force of five men will isolate the village communications-wise. They'll be able to see something of what will be going on, of course, but we don't anticipate any bother from them. All outgoing radio and telephone calls will be scrambled."

Miss Brunner looked up at Jerry Cornelius. "Do you

expect any trouble before we get into this cliff-opening place, Mr Cornelius?"

Jerry nodded.

"Boats about as big as your hoverlaunch, plus my own, are almost bound to be spotted. They've got radar. My guess is that my brother will still rely mainly on the traps in the maze and so on. But the house will have some other surprises. As I told you, we'll have to get to the main control room as soon as we can. That's in the centre of the house. Once there, we can shut it down, and it will be straight fighting until we have Frank. I estimate that if you keep him off his junk for a couple of hours, he'll tell you exactly where the microfilm is."

Miss Brunner said quietly, "So we must preserve Frank at all costs."

"Until you have your information, yes. Then I'll deal with him."

"You *do* sound vengeful, Mr Cornelius." Miss Brunner smiled at him. Jerry shrugged and turned to the window again.

"There seems little else to discuss." Mr Smiles offered them all his cigarettes. "We have an hour or two to kill."

"Nearly three hours to kill, if we're leaving at five," said Miss Brunner.

"Is it three hours?" Mr Powys glanced about.

"Three hours," said Mr Crookshank, nodding and looking at his watch. "Almost."

"What's the exact time?" Mr Smiles asked. "My watch seems to have stopped."

• • • • •

"I see that lire are thirty cents a million." Mr Crookshank lit Miss Brunner's cigarette with a large gold gas lighter.

"They should never have backed out of the Common Market," Miss Brunner said pitilessly.

"What else could they do?"

"The mark's still strong," said Mr Powys.

"Ah, the Russo-American mark. They can't go on supporting it at this rate." Mr Smiles smiled a satisfied smile. "No, indeed."

"I'm still not sure that we were in the right." Mr Powys sounded as if he were still not sure of anything. He glanced enquiringly towards the Scotch on the sideboard. Mr Smiles waved a hostly hand towards it. Mr Powys got up and poured himself a stiff one. "Refusing to pay back all those European loans, I mean. I think."

"It wasn't exactly a refusal," Dimitri reminded him. "You just asked for an indefinite time limit. Britain certainly is the black sheep of the family today, isn't she?"

"It can't be helped, and if we're lucky tonight, it will all be to our advantage in the long run." Mr Smiles rubbed his beard and walked to the sideboard. "Would anyone like a drink?"

"Yes, please," said Mr Powys.

The rest accepted, too, except for Jerry, who continued to look out of the window.

"Mr Cornelius?"

"What?" Dimitri glanced up. "Sorry." Mr Powys gave

him a baffled look. He held a glass of Scotch in each hand. Miss Brunner glared at Dimitri.

"I'll have a small one." Jerry appeared not to have noticed Dimitri's mistake, though, as he took the glass from Mr Smiles, he grinned broadly for a moment.

"Oh, we are living in an odd kind of limbo, aren't we?" Ever since the weary lemming image had occurred to him, Mr Crookshank had retained his philosophical mood. "Society hovers on the point of collapse, eh? Chaos threatens!"

Mr Powys had begun trying to pour one full glass of Scotch into the other. Whisky ran onto the carpet.

Cornelius felt that Mr Powys was overdoing it a bit. He smiled a little as he sat down on the arm of Miss Brunner's chair. Miss Brunner shifted in the chair, trying to face him and failing.

"Maybe the West has got to the quasar stage—you know, 3C286 or whatever it is." Miss Brunner spoke rapidly, half angrily, leaning away from Jerry Cornelius.

"What's that?" Mr Powys sucked his fingers.

"Yes, what is it?" Mr Crookshank seemed to dismiss Mr Powys's question as he asked his identical one.

"Quasars are quasi-stellar objects," Jerry said, "so massive that they've reached the stage of gravitational collapse."

"What's that got to do with the West?" Mr Smiles asked. "Astronomy?"

"The more massive, in terms of population, an area becomes, the more mass it attracts, until the state of gravitational collapse is reached," Miss Brunner explained.

"Entropy, I think, Mr Crookshank, rather than chaos," Jerry said kindly.

Mr Crookshank smiled and shook his head. "You're going a bit beyond me, Mr Cornelius." He looked around at the others. "Beyond all of us, I should say."

"Not beyond me." Miss Brunner spoke firmly.

"The sciences are becoming curiously interdependent, aren't they, Mr Cornelius?" said Dimitri, whose statement seemed to echo one he'd picked up earlier. "History, physics, geography, psychology, anthropology, ontology. A Hindu I met—"

"I'd love to do a programme," said Miss Brunner.

"I don't think there's a computer for the job," Jerry said.

"I intend to do a programme," she said, as if she'd made up her mind on the spot.

"You'd have to include the arts, too," he said. "Not to mention philosophy. It could be just a matter of time, come to think of it, before all the data crystallised into something interesting."

"Of Time?"

"That, too."

Miss Brunner smiled up at Jerry. "We have something in common. I hadn't quite realised what."

"Oh, only our ambivalence," Jerry grinned again.

"You're in a good mood," said Mr Powys suddenly to Jerry.

"I've got something to do," Jerry answered, but Mr Powys was staring at his Scotch again.

Miss Brunner felt extremely satisfied. She returned

to the subject. "I'd like more information. You know that this computer could be built. And what would it, in turn, create? Where are we heading?"

"Towards permanent flux perhaps, if you'll forgive the paradox. Not many would have the intelligence to survive. When Europe's finally divvied up between the Russians and Americans—not in my lifetime, I hope— what expertise the survivors will have! Won't they be valuable to their new masters, eh? You should remember that, Miss Brunner, if ever events look like exceeding their present speed." Jerry tapped her playfully on the shoulder.

She reached up to touch his hand, but it had gone. He got up.

"Can Time exceed c?" She laughed. "I'm sliding off, Mr Cornelius. But we must take up this conversation again."

"Now or never," he said. "Tomorrow I'll be away, and we shan't meet again."

"You're very certain."

"I have to be." He no longer grinned as he went back to the window, remembering Catherine and what he must do to Frank.

Behind him, the conversation continued.

Miss Brunner was in a savage, exhilarated mood now.

"And what's your philosophy for the coming Light Age, Mr Powys? You know, the c age. That's a better term, on second thoughts."

"Second thoughts?" Mr Powys could summon

nothing else. He was now on his fifth thought, trying to equate it with his fourth and, as he remembered it, his third "vasectomy".

Mr Powys was busily disintegrating.

Mr Smiles kindly filled his glass up, there being some good in all of us.

4

Jerry steered the boat towards the light that had suddenly flashed out from a point near his port. Illuminated by the greenish glow from his indicator panel, his face looked stranger than ever to the others who waited on the deck outside his cabin.

Miss Brunner, most prone to that sort of thing, reflected that the conflicting time streams of the second half of the twentieth century were apparently mirrored in him, and it seemed that the mind behind cried forward while the mind in front cried back.

What had Cornelius been getting at? Time disintegrating? She'd never read one of his books, but she'd heard of them. Didn't some of them talk about cyclical time, like Dunne? The ultimate point in the future. But what if something interrupted the cycle? An historical event, perhaps, of such importance that the whole pattern was changed. The nature of time, assuming that it was cyclical, would be disrupted. The circle broken, what might happen? It would certainly make Spengler look silly, she thought, amused.

If she could get her computer built and start her other project as well, she might be the person who could save something from the wreckage. She could consolidate everything left into one big programme—the final programme, she thought. Idea and reality, brought together, unified. The attempt had never succeeded in the past; but now she might have the opportunity to do it, for the time seemed ripe. She would need more power and more money, but with a bit of luck and intelligent exploitation of a shaky world situation she could get both.

Jerry was bringing the boat up alongside the bigger hoverlaunch. He watched as his passengers boarded the vessel, but he didn't join them, preferring to have his own boat waiting for him when the expedition was over.

The hoverlaunch whispered away towards Normandy, and he began to follow behind it, positioning his boat slightly to one side to avoid the main disturbance of the launch's wake. The launch belonged to Mr Smiles, who, like Jerry, had invested his money in tangibles while it had still had some value.

Bit by bit the Normandy coastline became visible. Jerry cut his engine, and the hoverlaunch followed suit. Jerry went out on deck as a line was shot to him from the hoverlaunch. He made it fast. It was a cold night.

The hoverlaunch started up again, with Jerry in tow. It headed towards the cliff where the fake Le Corbusier château stood, a silhouette in the moonlight.

There was a slight chance that the bigger boat wouldn't register on the mansion's radar. Jerry's boat didn't, but it was much lower in the water. The hoverlaunch's central control bridge, a squat tube rising above the passenger disc and power section, was what might just blip on the radar.

Old Cornelius's microfilms were buried deep within the château, in a strongroom that would not resist a high-explosive blast but would, if attacked in this manner, automatically destroy the film.

The information the intrepid band required was probably there, but the only sure-fire means of getting the film was to open the strongroom in the conventional way, and that was why Frank, who knew the various codes and techniques necessary, had to be preserved and questioned and, with luck, made to open the strongroom himself.

The whole house was designed around the strongroom. It had been built to protect the microfilms. Very little in the house was what it seemed to be. It was armed with strange weapons.

As he looked up at it, Jerry thought how strongly the house resembled his father's tricky skull.

Virtually every room, every passage, every alcove had booby traps, which was why Jerry was so valuable to the expedition. He didn't know the strongroom combination, but he knew the rest of the house well, having been brought up there.

If he hadn't gone off after that night when his father had found him with Catherine, he would have inherited the microfilms as his birthright, since he was the elder son, but Frank had got that honour.

The wind was up. It whistled through the trees, groaned among the towers of the château. The clouds ripped across the sky to reveal the moon.

The hoverlaunch rocked.

From the house, searchlights came on.

The searchlights were focused mainly on the house itself, lighting it up like some historic monument—which, indeed, it was.

The lights blinked off, and then another one came on, a powerful beam, moving across the water. It struck the hoverlaunch.

The other lights came on, concentrated on the house, particularly the roof.

Jerry shouted, "Keep your eyes off the roof! Don't look at the towers! Remember what I told you!"

Water splashed against the sides of the hoverlaunch as they waited.

From the roof three circular towers had risen. They began to rotate in the blue beam of a searchlight. The colour changed to red, then yellow, then lilac. The towers rotated slowly at first. They looked like big round machine-gun bunkers, with slots located at intervals down their length. Through these oblong slots shone bright lights, geometric shapes in garish primary colours, fizzing like neon. The towers whirled faster. It was almost impossible to take the eye away.

Jerry Cornelius knew what the giant towers were.

Michelson's Stroboscope Type 8. The eye was trapped by them and so were the limbs, the will. Pseudo-epilepsy was only one result of watching them for too long.

The wind and the hissing towers produced a high-pitched, ululating whine. Round and round, faster and faster, whirled the towers, with bright metal colours replacing the primaries—silver, bronze, gold, copper, steel.

First the eye and then the mind, thought Jerry.

He saw that one of the mercenaries on the boat stood transfixed; glazed, unblinking eyes staring up at the huge stroboscopes. His limbs were stiff.

A searchlight found him, and, from two concrete emplacements on the cliff, machine guns smacked a couple of dozen rounds into him.

His bloody body was thrown violently backward; it softened and collapsed. Jerry was still yelling at him to take his eyes away from the stroboscopes.

Jerry stopped yelling. He hadn't expected such a display of violence so soon. Evidently Frank wasn't taking chances. He crouched behind the cabin as the boats drifted towards the cliffs. The overhang offered them some shelter.

Within a minute the towers were no longer visible. They had been designed primarily for use against land attack.

As his boat bumped against the hoverlaunch, Jerry glanced at the body of the dead mercenary. It represented the start of an interesting anarchic process.

He leaned over and got a grip on a handrail, hauling himself aboard the hoverlaunch. He took out his needle gun and held it in his gloved right hand.

"Welcome aboard, Mr Cornelius," said Miss Brunner, her legs astraddle, her hair blowing back from her head.

Jerry walked forward as the hoverlaunch knocked itself against the cliff. Behind him a mercenary jumped to the deck of his boat and made it fast.

Another mercenary—darkly tanned, with oiled, wavy hair—came forward holding a suction mine intended to destroy the door. The man steadied himself and bent to attach it to the spot Jerry indicated. They backed up the deck as the mine exploded, bits of wreckage pattering down.

The door was open.

Jerry led the way forward, put his foot on the handrail and pushed himself into the opening. He began to walk down the short passage.

The main force of mercenaries, dressed in the light-weight khaki they were never without, followed him with their machine guns ready. Behind them, not so swiftly, stepped Mr Smiles, Miss Brunner and Dimitri, Mr Crook-shank and Mr Powys. They all carried their big machine pistols awkwardly.

An explosion rocked the cliff. They looked back as fire spread over the water.

"Let's hope they don't spend too much time on the boats," Mr Smiles said, speaking adenoidally because his nostrils were stuffed with the filters that Jerry had issued to them all.

Jerry reached the inner room and pointed at two places on the walls. The leading mercenary raised his gun and shot out the two cameras. From the control chamber above, the lights were switched off by way of retaliation.

"Frank's found this entrance, anyway," Jerry said. It was really only what he'd expected.

The mercenaries now unhooked heavy helmets from their belts and fitted them on their heads. The helmets were equipped with miners' lamps. One mercenary had a long coil of nylon rope over his shoulder.

"Perhaps the lift's still working?" Mr Powys suggested as Jerry set foot on the ladder.

"Probably." Jerry began to climb. "But we'd look great if they switched the power off when we were halfway up."

They all started to climb. Miss Brunner went last. As she put her foot on the first rung, she said thoughtfully, "Silly. They forgot to electrify the ladder."

Jerry heard some sounds above. He looked up as a light went on in the shaft, making him blink. A hard-faced German was looking down at him, sighting along his automatic rifle.

Jerry snapped up his needle gun and shot the German full of steel. He paused, arm curled around the ladder, to repressure the gun, shouting "Look out!" as the guard rolled off the edge and fell down the shaft.

As the guard's body thumped to the bottom, Jerry reached the top, his needle gun ready, but no-one was there. Frank had spared only one guard here, being sure that the maze would serve him best.

Everyone else scrambled up, and they all stood at the entrance to the maze while the soldier with the rope paid it out to them. They roped up.

Knotting her bit of the rope around her waist, Miss Brunner looked uncomfortable.

"I don't like this sort of thing," she said.

Jerry ignored her, leading them into the maze.

"Keep your mouths tightly shut," he reminded them. "And whatever happens, keep your attention on following me."

Their helmet lights lit the way as Jerry walked cautiously ahead, pointing out television cameras to the mercenaries, who shot them as they passed.

Then the first wave of gas hissed into the passageway. It was LSD gas, refined by old Cornelius. The nose filters, sophisticated by his son, could cope with it if they got through it fast enough. Old Cornelius had invented or modified all the hallucinatory protective devices in the house. Frank had added the guns and guards.

Hallucinogenic gases had been old Cornelius's speciality, though an offshoot had been his hallucimats such as the rooftop stroboscopic towers.

Old Cornelius had exhausted and killed himself searching for the ultimate hallucinogenic device ("total dissociation in under one second" had been his aim, his war-cry), just as his son Frank was destroying himself fairly slowly by looking for the ultimate kick in the veins.

Someone began to giggle, and Jerry looked back.

Mr Powys had his arms high and was shaking all over, just as if someone were tickling his armpits. Every so often he would stretch out his arms in front of him and make pushing motions at wisps of gas.

Then he began to skip about.

Mouths thin and firm now that they had seen the example of Mr Powys, Mr Smiles and Mr Crookshank stepped in, striving to hold him still.

Jerry signed for the expedition to stop, unhooked the rope from his belt, and went back to hit Mr Powys on the back of the neck with his pistol barrel.

Mr Powys relaxed, and Mr Smiles and Mr Crookshank hefted him up between them.

In silence they walked on through the faintly yellowish gas that clouded the air of the maze. Those who had absorbed a little of it thought they saw shapes in the writhing stuff: malevolent faces, grotesque figures, beautiful designs. Everyone was sweating, particularly Mr Smiles and Mr Crookshank, who carried Mr Powys who would soon have breathed enough LSD to kill him.

At a junction Jerry hesitated, his judgement slightly impaired. Then he was off again, taking the gang down the tunnel that branched off to the right.

They moved on, the silence sometimes interrupted by the sound of a rifle shooting out a camera.

It was a little ironic, he thought, that his father should have become so obsessed with the problem of the increasing incidence of neurotic disorders in the world that he himself had gone round the bend towards the end.

Now Jerry rounded the last bend and the door of the control chamber was ahead of him. He was quite surprised that so far there had been only two casualties and only one of those actually dead.

About fifteen yards before they got to the door Jerry gave a signal, and a bazooka was passed down the line to him. Leaving Jerry and his loader, the remainder of the party retreated down the passage a short way and stood in a disorderly knot waiting.

Jerry got the bazooka comfortably onto his shoulder and pulled the trigger. The rocket bomb whooshed straight through the door and exploded in the control room itself.

A booted foot came sailing out and hit Jerry in the face. He kicked it to one side, his mouth still tightly shut, and waved the others on.

The explosion had wrecked the control panel, but the opposite door was still intact. Since it would open only to the thermal code of someone it knew, they could either blast through into the library or wait for someone to blast through to them. Jerry knew that armed men would definitely be waiting in the library.

The other members of the expedition were unhooking their ropes and dropping them to the floor. It was unlikely they would be leaving by the same route, and therefore they wouldn't need the ropes again. Jerry pondered the problem as Miss Brunner squeezed into the room and studied the wreckage of the panel.

Her big eyes looked up at him quizzically. "A nice little board; and this is only a minor control panel?"

"Yes. There's a large roomful in the cellars—the main console. That's got to be our objective, as I told you."

"You did. What now?"

Jerry smoothed the hair at the side of his face.

"There's an alternative to waiting for them. We could try the bazooka. But there's another door behind this one, and I doubt if a rocket would go through them both. If it didn't, we'd get the worst of the explosion. They must be waiting there—probably with a grenade thrower or a big Bren or something. It's stalemate for the moment."

"You should have anticipated this." Miss Brunner frowned.

"I know."

"Why didn't you?"

"I didn't think of it," Jerry said with a sigh.

"Someone else should have." She turned to look accusingly at the others.

Dimitri was kneeling beside Mr Powys, trying to revive him. "You, too," he said. "Looks as if poor old Mr Powys has had it."

"I thought it had been too easy," said Mr Smiles.

"Not for Mr Powys," said Mr Crookshank, unable to restrain a slight smile. "The LSD always gets you in the end, eh?"

"I've got it." Jerry looked up. Over the door was a metal panel, secured by wing nuts. He pointed to it. "Air conditioning. A grenade thrower, a single neurade and a good eye should do the trick if the grille at the other end isn't closed."

He put his hand on the arm of a big South African. "You'll do. I'll stand on your shoulders. Hang on to my legs when the recoil comes. Who's got a grenade attachment?"

One of the Belgians handed him the attachment. He

fitted it to the automatic rifle and detached the ammunition clip. The Belgian handed him a different clip. He fitted this to the rifle, too. Then he took a neurade out of his pocket and popped it into the thrower's basket.

"Someone give me a hand up," he said. One of the British mercenaries helped him climb onto the South African's broad shoulders. He pushed back the metal panel and began to bash in the wire grille with the gun butt. He could see down the pipe to where the lights of the library shone. He heard muted voices.

Shoving the rifle into the pipe, he put it on his shoulder. The space between the fan blades was just big enough. Now if the neurade wasn't deflected by the grille at the other end, which wasn't likely, they'd have a chance of getting the guards there in silence and have time to blast open the doors with small charges of explosive before anyone realised that the detachment in the library was out of action.

He squeezed the trigger. The neurade shot down the pipe, was missed by the fan blades, and burst through the grille.

He smiled as voices at the other end shouted in surprise. He heard dull thumps and knew that the neurade had exploded. Then he started to lose his footing on the South African; half-jumped, half-fell to the ground; and handed the Belgian's gun back to him.

"Okay, let's get these doors open. Hurry. And keep your mouths closed again."

The charges burst both locks, and they were through. On the floor of the library beside an overturned machine

gun three Germans jerked limply, mouths in rictus grins, eyes full of tears, muscles and limbs contorted as the gas worked on their nerves. It seemed a mercy to bayonet them; so they did.

They tumbled out of the library and into the ground-floor hall as the ceiling suddenly rose and the walls widened out, light glaring like magnesium, blinding them for a moment. Jerry fished goggles from his pocket and put them on, noticing that the others were doing the same.

They could now see shapes flickering around them, like a colour-film negative. Traceries of deep red and luminous blue veined the walls.

Then the lights went out and they were in pitch-blackness.

One wall became transparent all at once. Behind it a huge black-and-white disc began to whirl, and a rhythmic boom swam up the decibel scale, almost to pain level. It seemed that the enlarged room swayed like a ship as they staggered after Jerry, who was none too steady on his pins himself, heading straight for the disc.

Jerry grabbed a gun from one of the dazed, mesmerised mercenaries, switched it to full automatic, and fired an entire magazine into the wall. Plastic cracked, but the disc continued to whirl. As he turned to take another gun, Jerry saw that all of them were now transfixed by the disc.

Another burst and the plastic shattered. The bullets struck the disc, and it began to slow down.

Behind them the far wall slid upwards, and half a dozen of Frank's guards stood there.

Jerry ignored them as he kicked a larger hole in the wall and smashed at the big disc with his gun butt until it crumpled.

"Throw down your arms!" ordered the chief guard.

Jerry flung himself through the hole. Aiming between Miss Brunner and Dimitri, who were beginning to blink back into wakefulness, he killed the chief guard.

The shot seemed to be enough to bring the others round quickly. Almost before Jerry knew it Miss Brunner had jumped through the hole, her high heels catching him on his buttocks.

Firing broke out generally, but Mr Smiles, Dimitri and Mr Crookshank all got through safely, although several of the mercenaries, including the big South African, died.

They fought back until they had killed all Frank's guards. It was fairly easy from their cover.

They were in a small room, now bathed in a soft red

light, a sound like the swish of the sea in their ears.

Something dropped from the ceiling and bounced on the floor until its sides opened up.

"Nerve bomb!" Jerry yelled. "Cover your mouths!"

He knew there was an exit somewhere to the right of the smashed disc. He edged in that direction and found it, using his gun to prise it open. If they didn't get out shortly, their nose filters wouldn't help them.

He went through the doorway, and they followed him.

The next room was yellow, full of soothing murmurs. A remote-control camera panned around close to the roof. One of the mercenaries shot it. A normal door, unlocked, opened onto a flight of stairs leading upward.

There wasn't another door. They ascended the stairs. At the top three men waited for them.

"Frank's spreading his guards thin," said Jerry.

Their first burst missed him but shot the head of one of the Belgians to bits. Feeling panicky, Jerry hugged the wall, raising his needle gun and shooting a guard in the throat.

Behind him the leading mercenaries opened up. One guard fell at once, blood spurting from his stomach. The second fired down the stairwell and got two more mercenaries, including one of the Britons.

Jerry, rapidly repressuring his gun, shot him, too.

On the first-floor landing everything was silent, and Jerry relaxed his pursed lips. The mercenaries, with the civilians behind them, moved up onto the landing and looked at him questioningly.

"My brother's almost certainly in the main control

room," Jerry said. "That's two floors down now, and there'll be extra guards turning up at any moment." Jerry pointed at a television camera near the ceiling. "Don't shoot it. He isn't using it at the moment for some reason, and if we put it out he'll know we're here."

"He must have guessed, surely," said Miss Brunner.

"You'd think so. Also, he would have sent some reinforcements here by now. He could have a trap waiting somewhere for us—wants us to relax a little. This landing's equipped with a Schizomat in a panel in that wall. My father's crowning achievement, he always thought."

"And Frank isn't using it." Miss Brunner tidied her long red hair.

"I had to leave Mr Powys behind, I'm afraid." Dimitri leaned on a wall. "This house certainly is full of colourful surprises, Mr Cornelius."

"He'll be dead by now," said Jerry.

"What could your brother be planning?" Miss Brunner asked.

"Something funny. He's got a rich sense of humour. He may have cooked up a new ploy, but it's not like Frank to be subtle at a time like this. It's just possible that he's run away."

"And all our efforts have been wasted," she said sourly. "I hope not."

"Oh, so do I, Miss Brunner."

He walked along the landing, with them following him. Jerry led them through the quiet house until they reached a point where they looked down, through what was evidently a two-way mirror, into the partitioned hall where the nerve bomb had exploded. Stairs led down alongside the far wall.

"These stairs normally lead to the basement," Jerry told them. "We might as well go back the way we came now. There's no obvious danger as far as I can see."

They began to descend.

"There are steel gates further down," he said. "They can shut off any part of the stairs. Remember what I told you: use your guns to wedge them, stop them fully closing."

"No rifle's going to stop steel," Mr Crookshank said doubtfully.

"True—but the door mechanism's delicate. It'll work."

They passed openings in the walls where the steel gates were housed, but none of them closed.

They reached the ground floor and entered a curiously narrow passage, obviously created by the widening of the hall walls earlier. At the far end Mr Powys suddenly appeared and came staggering towards them.

"He should be dead!" exclaimed Mr Smiles, offended.

"It's haunted! It's haunted!" moaned Mr Powys.

Jerry couldn't work out how he'd got there. Neither could he guess how Mr Powys had survived the LSD, not to mention everything else.

"It's haunted! It's haunted!" Mr Powys repeated.

Jerry grabbed him. "Mr Powys! Pull yourself together."

Mr Powys gave Jerry an intelligent look that was suddenly sardonic. He raised his thick eyebrows. "Too late for that, I'm afraid, Mr Cornelius. This house—it's like a giant head. Do you know what I mean? Or is it *my* skull? If it is, what am I?"

"I know whose bloody head this house is," Jerry said, shaking him. "I know, you bastard!"

"Mine."

"No!"

"What's the matter, Mr Powys?" Dimitri slid up. "Can I help?"

"It's haunted. It's my mind haunted by me, I think. That can't really be right, Dimitri. You are Dimitri. I'd always thought… It must be my mind haunting me. That must be it. Oh, dear!" He rocked his poor head in his hands.

Dimitri looked at Jerry Cornelius. "What do we do with him?"

"He needs a converter." Jerry Cornelius smiled at Mr Powys, raised his gun and shot him in the eye.

The party stopped.

5

"It was for the best," Jerry said. "His brain was already badly damaged, and we couldn't have him running around."

"Aren't you being exceptionally ruthless, Mr Cornelius?" Mr Smiles took a very deep breath.

"Oh, now, now, Mr Smiles."

They pressed on until they reached a big metal door in the basement. "This is where he should be," said Jerry. "But I can't help thinking he's cooked up a big surprise." He signalled to the surviving Briton and a couple of Belgians. They saluted smartly.

"Have a go at that door, will you?"

"Any particular method, sir?" asked the Briton.

"No. Just get it down. We'll be round the corner."

They retreated while the soldiers got to work fixing things to the door.

There came a loud and unexpectedly violent explosion (obviously far bigger than the soldiers had planned). When the smoke cleared, Jerry saw blood all over the walls, but very little of the soldiers.

"Great lads," he laughed. "What a good thing, their thing about orders." And then they were all stumbling backward as a sub-machine gun began to bang rapidly from within the room.

Peering through the smoke from behind the cover of a South African, Jerry saw that Frank was in there, apparently alone, with the machine gun cradled in his arms, firing steadily.

Mr Crookshank got in the path of one of the bursts, making a ludicrous attempt to duck the bullets even as they danced into his chest. Two soldiers collapsed on top of him.

Frank chuckled away as he fired.

"I think he's gone barmy," said Mr Smiles. "This poses a problem, Mr Cornelius."

Jerry nodded. "Stop this nonsense, Frank!" he shouted, trying to make his tone firm. "What about a truce?"

"Jerry!

"Jerry!

"Jerry!" sang Frank from the room, firing more sporadically. "What do you want, Jerry? A Time Fix? Deep…

"Tempodex is my remedy for everyone. It'll turn you on lovely, sport—can't you feel those millions of years just waiting in your spine—waiting to move up into your back-brain—"

The gun stopped altogether and they began to move cautiously forward. Then Frank stooped to pick up an identical, fully loaded weapon. He began emptying it.

"—your mid-brain, your fore-brain—all your many brains, Jerry—when the tempodex starts opening them up?"

"He is in a jolly mood," said Miss Brunner from somewhere well behind the front line.

Jerry just didn't feel like doing anything except duck bullets at that moment. He felt very tired. Another couple of mercenaries piled themselves up neatly. They were running out of help, Jerry thought.

"Can't we throw something at him? Isn't there any more gas?" Miss Brunner sounded vexed.

"Well, look here, he's got to run out of bullets sooner or later." Mr Smiles believed that if you waited long enough, the right situation always presented itself. A thought struck him, and he turned angrily to the mercenaries. "Why aren't you retaliating?"

They began retaliating.

Mr Smiles quickly realised his mistake and shouted: "Stop! We want him alive!"

They stopped.

Frank sang and kept his finger on the trigger.

"He'll get an overheated barrel if he's not careful," said Mr Smiles, remembering his mythology. "I hope he doesn't blow himself up."

Miss Brunner was picking her nose. She discarded the filters. "I don't care if there is any more gas," she said, "I'm not having the filthy things up there any longer."

"Well, look," said Jerry, "I've got one neurade left, but it could kill him, the state he's in."

"It wouldn't do *me* much good now. You might have warned me." Miss Brunner scanned the floor.

Another mercenary groaned and went down.

The sub-machine gun stopped. The last bullet ricocheted off the wall. There came the sound of sobbing.

Jerry peered round the corner. Among his guns, Frank sat weeping with his head in his hands.

"He's all yours." Jerry walked towards the stairs.

"Where are you going?" Miss Brunner took a step after him.

"I've done my bit of group effort, Miss Brunner. Now there's something else I've got to do. Goodbye."

Jerry went up to the ground floor and found the front door. He still felt nervous and realised that not all Frank's guards had been accounted for. He opened the door and peered out of the house. There didn't seem to be anyone about.

Gun still in his hand, he walked down the sloping drive towards the lodge where John ought to be with Catherine.

The lights were out in the lodge, but he didn't think it strange in the circumstances. He looked down the hill towards the village. All the lights were out there, too. Mr Smiles had paid someone to fuse the power supply. Jerry found the lodge door open and walked in.

In a corner, a bag of bones gave him a welcoming groan.

"John! Where's Catherine?"

"I got her here, sir. I—"

"But where is she now? Upstairs?"

"You said after ten, sir. I was here by eleven. Everything went smoothly. She was a weight. I'm dying, sir, I think."

"What happened?"

"He must have followed me." John spoke with increasing faintness. "I got her here… Then he came in with a couple of the men. He shot me, sir."

"And took her back to the house?"

"I'm sorry, sir…"

"So you should be. Did you hear where he was taking her?"

"He—said—putting her—back to—bed, sir…"

Jerry left the lodge and began to run up the drive. It was odd how normal the house looked from the outside.

He re-entered it.

On the ground floor he found the lift and discovered that it was still operating. He got in and went up to the sixth. He got out and ran to Catherine's bedroom. The door was locked. He kicked at it, but it wouldn't budge. He reached into his top pocket and fished out something that looked like a cigarette. Two thin wires were attached to it, leading to another object the size of a matchbox. He uncoiled the wires. He put the slim object into the keyhole of the door and walked backward a yard or so with the box in his hand.

It was actually a tiny detonator. He touched the wires to the detonator, and the explosive at the other end burst the lock with a flash.

He pushed at the wrecked door and walked in to find Frank already there.

Frank did not look at all well. In his right hand was a needle gun, twin to Jerry's. There were only two such guns; their father had had them made and given them one each.

"How did you get away?" Jerry asked Frank.

Frank's answer was not a direct one. He put his head on one side and stared at Jerry unblinkingly, looking like an old, sick vulture.

"Well, actually I was hoping to get *you*, Jerry. As it was I got all your military friends, though I think I missed some of the others. They're still wandering about, I think. I'm not sure why I bothered with the shooting—probably just because I enjoyed it. I feel much better now. But if you'd crossed into the room you'd have found that a couple—ha, ha—of my men were on either side of the door waiting for you. I was the bait, the bait to the trap."

Frank's head seemed to be sinking deeper and deeper into his shoulders as he talked, his whole body screwed up in a neurotic stoop. "You certainly made a good try at getting our sister, didn't you? Look—I've woken the sleeping beauty up."

Catherine, looking dazed, was propped on pillows.

She smiled when she saw Jerry. It was a sweet smile, but it wasn't all that confident. Her skin was more than naturally pale, and her dark hair was still tangled.

Jerry's gun hand rose a trifle, and Frank grinned. "Let's get ready, then," he said.

He began to back around the bed in order to get on the other side of Catherine. She was now between them, looking slowly from one to the other, her smile fading very gradually.

Jerry was trembling. "You bastard."

Frank giggled. "That's something we all have in common."

Frank's junkie face was immobile. The only movement in it came when the light caught his bright, beady eyes. Jerry didn't realise that Frank had pulled the trigger of his gun until he felt the sting in his shoulder. Frank's hand wasn't as steady as it had seemed.

Frank didn't repressure his gun at once. Jerry raised his arm to shoot Frank.

Then Catherine moved. She reached out towards Frank, her fingers clutching at his coat. "Stop it!"

"Shut up," said Frank. He moved his left hand towards the pressure lever of his needle gun.

Catherine tried to stand up on the bed and fell forward in a kneeling position. Her face was full of wild fear.

"Jerry!" she screamed.

Jerry took a step towards her.

"That needle could work into your heart, Jerry," smiled Frank.

"So I'll need a magnet."

Jerry fired and ran towards the window as a needle grazed his face. He repressured and turned. Frank ducked; Catherine rose, and Jerry's needle caught her. She collapsed. Jerry repressured and discharged another needle at the same time as Frank. They both missed again.

Jerry began to feel puzzled. This was going on far too long. He jumped towards Frank and grabbed at his body. Frank's weak fists struck him on the head and back. He punched Frank in the stomach, and Frank groaned. They stepped apart. Jerry felt dizzy; saw Frank grin and wheel.

"You had something in those needles…"

"Find out," grinned Frank, and he sprang from the room.

Jerry sat himself down on the edge of the bed.

He was riding a black Ferris wheel of emotions. His brain and body exploded in a torrent of mingled ecstasy and pain. Regret. Guilt. Relief. Waves of pale light flickered. He fell down a never-ending slope of obsidian rock surrounded by clouds of green, purple, yellow, black. The rock vanished, but he continued to fall. World of phosphorescence drifting like golden spheres into the black night. Green, blue, red explosions. Flickering world of phosphorescent tears falling into timeless, spaceless wastes. World of Guilt. Guilt—guilt—guilt… Another wave flowed up his spine. No-mind, no-body, no-where. Dying waves of light danced out of his eyes and away through the dark world. Everything was dying. Cells, sinews, nerves, synapses—all crumbling. Tears of light, fading, fading. Brilliant rockets streaking into the sky and exploding all together and sending their multicoloured globes of light—balls on an Xmas tree—x-mass—drifting slowly. Black mist swirled across a bleak, horizonless nightscape. Catherine. As he approached her she fell away, fell down like a cardboard dummy. Just before his mind cleared, he thought he saw a creature bending over them both—a creature without a navel, hermaphrodite and sweetly smiling…

He felt weaker as his head cleared, and he realised that some time must have passed. Catherine lay on the bed in much the same position in which he'd seen her earlier. There was a spot of blood on her white dress, over the left breast.

He put his hand on it and noticed that the heart wasn't beating.

He had killed her.

In agony, he began to caress her stiff.

Meanwhile, Frank was also in agony, for he had been trapped by Miss Brunner and she was giving his genitals a cruel squeeze. They were in one of the rooms on the second floor. Dimitri and Mr Smiles stood at his left and right, holding his arms.

Miss Brunner knelt on one knee in front of him. She squeezed again, and Frank grimaced.

"Look here," he said. "I've got to get myself fixed up."

"You get the fix when we get the microfilm," snarled Miss Brunner, hoping he wouldn't give in right away.

Smiles got the joke and laughed. Dimitri joined in, somewhat vacantly.

"This is serious," said Miss Brunner, and she gave Frank another squeeze.

"I'll tell you as soon as I'm fixed up."

"Mr Cornelius, we can't allow that," said Mr Smiles. "Come along, let's have the information."

Mr Smiles hit Frank clumsily on the face. Discovering a taste for it, he did it several more times. Frank didn't seem to mind. He had other things to worry about.

"Pain doesn't have much effect," Miss Brunner said thoughtfully. "We'll just have to wait and hope he doesn't become too incoherent."

"Look, he's slavering." Dimitri pointed in disgust. He let go of Frank's arm.

Eyes unblinking, Frank wiped his grey mouth. A great shudder brought his body briefly to life. Then he was still again.

After a moment, while they watched in curiosity, he shuddered again.

"You know the microfilm is in the strongroom?" Frank said between shudders.

"He's coming through!" Mr Smiles smacked his leg.

"Only you can open the strongroom; is that right, Mr Cornelius?" Miss Brunner sighed rather disappointedly.

"That's right."

"Will you take us there and open the strongroom? Then we will let you go and you can get your fix."

"Yes, I will."

Mr Smiles bent Frank's arm behind his back. "Lead the way," he said firmly.

• • • • •

When they had reached the strongroom and Frank had opened it for them, Miss Brunner looked at the ranks of metal files lining the walls and said, "You can go now, Mr Cornelius. We'll find what we want."

Frank skipped off, out of the littered room behind the strongroom and up the stairs.

"I think I'll just pop after him and check he hasn't got something up his sleeve," Mr Smiles said eagerly.

"We'll be waiting."

Dimitri helped Miss Brunner lift the files from their shelves and cart them into the room. When Mr Smiles had disappeared, Miss Brunner began to stroke Dimitri. "We've done it, Dimitri!"

Dimitri had soon forgotten the boxes and had become totally absorbed in Miss Brunner.

Mr Smiles came back a short time later, looking upset. "I was right," he said. "He's left the house and is talking to his guards. We should have kept him as a hostage. We're not behaving very rationally, Miss Brunner."

"This isn't the time or place for that sort of thing," she said as she searched through the box files.

"Where's Mr Cornelius?"

"Jerry Cornelius?" she murmured abstractly.

"Yes."

"We should have asked Frank. Silly of me."

"Where's Dimitri?"

"He gave up."

"Gave himself up?" Mr Smiles looked bemused. He glanced round the strongroom. On the floor, in a dark corner, lay a neatly folded Courrèges suit, a shirt, underpants, socks, shoes, tie, valuables.

"Well, he must have gone for an early-morning swim," said Mr Smiles, trembling and noticing how healthy Miss Brunner's skin looked.

It was dawn as Jerry walked down the stairs. On the second floor he found Miss Brunner and Mr Smiles going through the big metal box files. They were sitting on the carpet with the files between them, studying the papers and microfilm they had removed.

"I assumed you were dead," said Miss Brunner. "We're the only survivors, I'm afraid."

"Where is Frank?"

"We let him go after he'd opened the strongroom for us. It was a mistake." She looked petulantly at Mr Smiles. "They aren't here, are they?"

Mr Smiles shook his head. "It doesn't look like it, Miss Brunner. We've been fooled by young Frank. At the rate he was trembling and drooling, you'd have thought he was telling the truth. He's more cunning than we guessed."

"Instinctive," said Miss Brunner, her lips pursed.

"What happened to Dimitri?" Jerry looked at Miss Brunner. For a moment, in the dawn light, he had half-mistaken her for the Greek.

"He disappeared," said Mr Smiles. "After I went to

check on Frank. I didn't realise the strength of character your brother had, Mr Cornelius."

"You shouldn't have let him go." Jerry kicked at the papers.

"You told us we mustn't harm him."

"Did I?" Jerry spoke listlessly now.

"I'm not sure he *was* lying," said Miss Brunner to Mr Smiles. She got up, dusting off her skirt as best she could. "He might really have believed the stuff was in there. Do you think it exists any more?"

"I was convinced. Convinced." Mr Smiles sighed. "A lot of time, energy and money has been wasted, and we're not even likely to survive now. This is a great disappointment."

"Why not?" Jerry asked. "Likely to survive?"

"Outside, Mr Cornelius, is the remainder of your brother's private army. They've ringed the place and are ready to shoot us. Your brother commands them."

"I must get to a doctor," said Jerry.

"What's the matter?" Miss Brunner's voice wasn't sympathetic.

"I'm wounded in a couple of places. One in the shoulder—not sure where the other one went in, but I think it must be very bad."

"What about your sister?"

"My sister's dead. I shot her."

"Really, then you must—"

"I want to live!" Jerry stumbled towards the window and looked out into the cold morning. Men were waiting there, though Frank couldn't be seen. The grey bushes seemed made of delicately carved granite, and grey gulls wheeled in a grey sky.

"By Christ, I want you to live, too!" Miss Brunner grasped him. "Can you think of a way we can all get out?"

"There is a chance." He began to speak calmly. "The main control chamber wasn't destroyed, was it?"

"No—perhaps we should have…"

"Let's get down there. Come on, Mr Smiles."

Jerry sat limply in the chair by the control board. He checked first that the power was on; then he activated the monitors so that they had a view all round the house. He locked the monitors on the armed men who were waiting outside.

His hand reached for another bank of switches and flipped them over. "We'll try the towers," he said.

Green, red and yellow lights went on above the board. "They're working, anyway." He stared carefully at the monitors. He felt very sick.

"Towers are spinning," he said. "Look!"

The armed men were all gaping at the roof. They could not have had any sleep all night, which would help the process. They stood transfixed.

"Get going," Jerry said as he got up and leaned on Mr Smiles, pushing him towards the door. "But once out of the house, don't look back or you'll be turned into a pillar of salt."

They helped him up the stairs. He was almost fainting

now. Cautiously, they opened the front door.

"Go, tiger!" he said weakly as they began to run, still supporting him.

"How are we going to get down to the boats?" asked Miss Brunner when they had helped him round the side of the house facing the cliff edge.

Jerry didn't care. "I suppose we'll have to jump," he murmured. "Hope the tide hasn't dropped too low."

"It's a long way down, and I'm not so sure I can swim." Mr Smiles slowed his pace.

"You'll have to try," said Miss Brunner.

They stumbled across the rough turf and got to the edge. Far below, water still washed the cliff. Behind them a strong-minded guard had spotted them. They could tell this because his bullets had begun to whine past them.

"Are you fit enough, Mr Cornelius?"

"I hope so, Miss Brunner."

They jumped together and fell together towards the sea.

Mr Smiles didn't follow them. He looked back, saw the stroboscopes, and could not turn away again. A smile appeared on his lips. Mr Smiles died smiling, at the hand of the strong-minded guard.

Jerry, now unaware of who or where he was, felt himself being dragged from the sea. Someone slapped his face. What, he wondered, was the nature of reality after all? Could all this be the result of mankind's will— even his natural surroundings, the shape of the hand that slapped his face?

"You're going to have to steer, I'm afraid, Mr Cornelius. I can't."

He smiled. "Steer? Okay." But what sort of place would he steer into? The world he had left? This world? Or another altogether? A world, perhaps, where killer girls roved metropolitan streets in bands, working for faceless tycoons who bought and sold hydrogen bombs on an international level, supplying the entire market with H— Hydrogen, Heroin, Heroines…

"Catherine," he murmured. Miss Brunner was kindly helping him to the cabin, he realised.

Tired but happy, unconvinced by the reality of his hallucination, he started the boat and swung out to sea.

Hi-Fi, Holiness, a hope in hell…

He would never have a memory of what happened until he cried "Catherine!" and woke to find that he was in a very comfortable hospital bed.

"If you don't mind my asking," he said politely to the lemon-faced woman in uniform who entered after a while, "where would I be?"

"You're in the Sunnydales Nursing Home, Mr Cornelius, and you are much better. On the way to recovery, they say. A friend brought you here after your accident at that French funfair."

"You know about that?"

"I know very little about it. Some trick gun went off the wrong way and shot you, I believe."

"Is that what happened? Are all nursing homes called Sunnydales?"

"Most of them."

"Am I receiving the very best medical attention?"

"You have had three specialists at your friend's expense."

"Who's the friend?"

"I don't know the name. The doctor might. A lady, I think."

"Miss Brunner?"

"The name's familiar."

"Will there be any complications? When will I be fit enough to leave?"

"I don't think any complications are expected. You will not leave until you are fit enough to do so."

"You have my word of honour—I shan't leave until I'm fit enough. My life's all I've got."

"Very wise. If there are any business matters you need arranging—any relatives?"

"I'm self-employed," he said self-consciously.

The nurse said, "Try getting some sleep."

"I don't need any sleep."

"You don't, but it's easier to run a hospital with all the patients sleeping. They're less demanding. Now you can do me a favour. Groan, beg for medical details, complain about the lack of attention we give you and the inferior way we run the hospital, but don't try to make me laugh."

"I don't think I could, could I?" said Jerry.

"It's a waste of time," she agreed.

"Then I wouldn't dream of it."

He felt fresh and relaxed and he wondered why he should, considering his recent activities. He'd probably have plenty of time in which to work it out. He knew he'd be fighting trauma on all fronts, and the long coma had equipped him to fight well.

As best he could, he began putting his mind in order. During the weeks in the hospital, all he asked for was a tape recorder, tape, and cans so that there would be no trouble when he turned up the sound in moments of heavy concentration.

PHASE

2

6

Better equipped for the world than before he'd arrived at the hospital, Jerry offered a grateful hand to the doctors who had saved him; gave the rest of the staff a graceful bow; got into his Duesenberg, which had been delivered from town; and drove through the weary streets of London's southernmost suburbs, heading for the important centre: the hot, bubbling core of the city.

He parked the car in the Shaftesbury Avenue garage he used and, stepping light, sallied out into his natural habitat.

It was a world ruled by the gun, the guitar and the needle, sexier than sex, where the good right hand had become the male's primary sexual organ, which was just as well considering that the world population had been due to double before the year 2000.

This wasn't the world Jerry had always known, but he could only vaguely remember a different one, so similar to this that it was immaterial which was which. The dates checked roughly, that was all he cared about, and the mood was much the same.

Recently converted from a cinema, jangling on thirteen fun-packed floors, Emmett's Coin Casino was the place to go, Jerry decided. He turned a corner and there it was.

Its three visible sides were entirely covered with neon of every possible colour: neon words and neon pictures with six or even ten different movements. And the music didn't blare out; it came out faint and flattened—soft, muted tones that really only suggested music.

An early-twentieth-century mystic might have thought he'd had a vision of heaven if he'd seen it, thought Jerry as he made his way slowly towards it.

It sparked and flashed, rolled and smoked, and high above everything else, seemingly suspended in the dark sky, was the single golden word EMMETTS.

At the coruscating entrance foyer, attended by young girls in military uniforms with imitation rifles with which they jokingly pretended to bar his way, Jerry changed a bundle of notes into a bag of counters for use in the fun machines. He went through the tall, shining red-and-blue turnstile and trod the thick, jazzy carpet into the first gallery, which was at ground level.

Beams of soft pastel light roamed through the semi-darkness of the hall, and money-operated machines clattered, spoke and sang. Jerry began to descend the short flight of steps, listening to the laughter of the young men and women who wandered among the machines, or lingered by them, or danced to the free music from the giant jukebox that filled the best part of one wall.

Jerry spent a few tokens on the Ray Range, operating a simulated laser beam that spat light at targets. If the ray of light struck a specified zone, you won a prize. But his score was low; he was out of practice. This spoiled his state of mind, and he began to think that if he hadn't worried so little about marksmanship, he wouldn't be in this mental limbo now. Catherine—or rather the lack of Catherine—had given his life the only dynamism it was likely to have. Now he lacked her for good. It was over.

Aimlessly, he wandered among the pin tables and fruit machines, bent over by happy young men who worked them excitedly, hand in hand. Jerry sighed and thought that the true aristocracy who would rule the seventies were out in force: the queers and the lesbians and the bisexuals, already half-aware of their great destiny which would be realised when the central ambivalence of sex would be totally recognised and the terms *male* and *female* would become all but meaningless. Here they were. As he wandered, he was surrounded by all the possible replacements for sex, one or several of which would become the main driving force for the humanity of circa 2000—light, colour, music, the pin tables, the pill dispensers, the gun ranges—scarcely substitutes for sex any more, but natural replacements.

The birth rate, which if it had continued at the speed predicted in the early sixties would have produced by 4000 a planet consisting, core and crust, of nothing but human beings, was a dead pigeon to modern statisticians in Europe. Europe as usual was ahead of the world.

Most of those who hadn't been able to stand the pace had emigrated off to America, Africa, Russia, Australia, and elsewhere where they could wallow in the nostalgia produced by American fashions and television shows and mass opinion, African rural life, Russian moral attitudes, and Australian cold mutton. The flow had been two-way, of course, with the passengers for 1950 going one way and the passengers for 2000 coming the other. Only France, Switzerland and Sweden, temporal and temporary bastions, hung back and stood soon to be shaken to pieces in the imminent pre-entropic wash of crisis. It was not a change of mood, Jerry thought, but a change of mind.

Jerry no longer had any idea whether the world he inhabited was "real" or "false"; he had long since given up worrying about it.

By the spinning Racette, where you could back a model horse named after your favourite winner of the season, Jerry met Shades, an acquaintance.

Shades was a killer from California who had once told Jerry that he could prove he'd assassinated both Kennedys. When Jerry, who had believed him, had asked why, Shades had replied rather self-consciously, "The thrill of big game, you know. I'd considered having a go at your Queen, but it wouldn't have been the same. I got the biggest. The world cried for Jack Kennedy, you know."

"And Valentino. You could have led up to him."

"No, if I'd done that the trauma wouldn't have been so great—people would have been half-ready. I got me the Sun King. What a charge. Oh, boy!"

"What did you do it with? Mistletoe?"

"An Italian Mauser," Shades had told him, offended by his levity.

Shades had two girls with him: a redhead of about sixteen and a brunette of about twenty-five. Shades's lamp-tanned face turned to grin at Jerry. He was naked apart from a pair of shorts and a bolero. His real clothing, his essential clothing, was his dark glasses. He looked out of place. The girls both wore tweed trouser suits. Their hair was short, and their green-highlighted make-up glinted under the coloured beams.

The older girl had a newssheet in her hand. Jerry looked at her. "You're Swedish?"

She didn't seem surprised at his guess. "Ja—and you?"

"No. I'm English."

"Ja so!"

Jerry leaned forward and took the sheet from the Swedish girl's hand. "Anything new lately?" He'd been wondering if the raid on the house had reached the sheets. It was unlikely.

"Britain's in some sort of debt," said the young girl. "It's something to do with the crime-rate doubling."

Jerry glanced over the sheet, then reversed it to look at the comics. Instead there was a photo covering the whole side: a mass car smash with mangled corpses everywhere. Jerry supposed that the picture sold sheets.

"Well, Shades," he said, handing the sheet back to the girl, "what are you up to these days?"

"Pianotron at the Friendly Bum. Why don't you come along and sit in?"

"Good idea."

"I'm not due till the third set around three. What do we do in the meantime?"

"Help me get rid of these tokens, then we'll talk about it."

The Swedish girl attached herself to Jerry, and they made a happy circuit of the tables. The girl chewed gum steadily, and Jerry was slightly put out by this, but was mollified as her little hand tentatively touched him up. It was a nice thought, he felt, as he restrained her.

A stooped old man passed between the tables. He had long white hair almost to his waist; a long white beard to match; a pink, soft skin; and a small briefcase under his arm. He was stooped almost horizontally, and his little pale blue eyes seemed as bright as the bulbs on the pin tables. He nodded at Jerry and stopped politely.

"Good evening, Mr Cornelius. We haven't seen much of you lately, or is it me who's been out of touch?" His voice was breathy.

"You're never out of touch, Derek. How's the astrology business?"

"Can't complain. Want a chart done?"

"I've had too many, Derek. You'll never work it out."

"There's something very odd there, you know. I've been doing charts for sixty years and never come up against one like yours. It's as if you didn't exist." His laugh was breathy, too.

"Come off it, Derek—you're only forty-six."

"Oh, you know that, do you? Well, thirty years, anyway."

"And you only took up astrology ten years ago. Just before you gave up your job in the Foreign Office."

"Who've you been talking to?"

"You."

"I don't always tell the truth, you know."

"No. Where's Olaf?"

"Oh, he's about." Derek looked sharply up at Jerry. "It wasn't you, was it?"

"What?"

"Olaf's left me. I taught him the lot. I loved him. And it's rare for a Sagittarian to love a Virgo, you know. Scorpios are all right. Olaf ran off with some crackpot star watcher I've never heard of. I just wondered. Do you know, when I first started up professionally there weren't more than six what you might call real astrologers moving around the way I do. Know how many there are now?"

"Six hundred."

"You're almost right. I can't count them all. On the other hand, custom's gone up. But not really proportionately."

"Don't worry, Derek. You're still the best."

"Well, spread it around. No, you see, I'd heard Olaf was here. I'm sure once he sees me—in the flesh, as it were—he'll realise his mistake."

"I'll keep my eyes open."

"Good lad." Derek patted Jerry's arm and sloped off.

"Is he very wise?" asked the Swedish girl.

"He's sharp," said Jerry. "And that's what matters."

"Every time," she said, taking his hand. He let her lead him back to where Shades was lying across a table with his nose pressed to the glass as little balls smacked against little coils and bounced about at random until they hit other little coils. Shades's hands gripped the edges of the table, and when a bell rang the knuckles whitened.

"*This* is what I call conditioning, Jerry," he said, not looking up. "Get a load of me. I'm Pavlov's poodle!"

"Let's see you dribble, you old-fashioned sweetie," Jerry smiled, taking it easy. He was relaxing now, moving with the tide. He pinched Shades's bottom, and Shades kicked backward with a low-heeled cowboy boot.

"You riding me?"

"Not tonight, honey."

This was more like it, thought Jerry, taking a deep breath of smoke, scent and incense. He felt on top again. Just on top of himself.

Shades laughed. He had been concentrating on the little steel balls.

Looking about, Jerry recognised Derek's Olaf having a go on the Killagal range. You had ten shots in which to knock down six out of ten life-size plastic nude girls with something made to look like a harpoon gun. He wasn't doing too well. Olaf was a slight, pinch-faced lad who gave the impression that someone had had him filleted. He put down the gun and went over to the machine that read palms. He put his money in and laid his palm limply on the section made of pulsating rubber. As Jerry approached, the machine cut off and a little card appeared in a slot. Olaf removed it and studied it. He frowned, shaking his head.

"Hello, Olaf. Derek's looking for you."

"That's none of your business." Olaf's voice was contentious and whining. It was his normal voice.

"No. Derek asked me to let him know if I saw you."

"I suppose you want something from me. Well, I just spent my last guinea, and I don't have anything to do with Arians."

"You're not a Jewish boy, are you?" Jerry said. "Don't mind my asking, but you're not, are you?"

"Shut up!" Olaf's voice stayed at the same pitch and tone, but became more precise. "I'm sick and tired of people like you."

"No offence, no offence, but…"

"Shut up!"

"I only thought, since you said…"

"You can't take the mickey out of me, you know." Olaf turned his back. Jerry skipped round and got in front of him again. "Now, *look*," said Olaf.

"Did anyone ever tell you had a beautiful body, Olaf?"

"Don't try to make up for it now," said Olaf, his voice becoming slightly less precise and a trifle softer. "Anyway, you're an Arian. I *can't* have anything to do with Arians. It would be disastrous."

"Got to keep pure, Olaf, eh?"

"Don't start that again. People like you are scum

from the lowest pits. You've got no understanding of what it's like to be a real, spiritual human being, *knowing* the infinite—" Olaf gave a thin, superior smile. "Scum from the lowest pits."

"That's what I mean. You don't *sound* like a Jewish boy."

"Shut up."

"All right—go and see Derek."

"I want nothing to do with that pervert!"

"Pervert? Why pervert?"

"It's nothing to do with *sex*—you see what I mean about having no understanding?—it's to do with his ideas. He's perverted the whole science of astrology. Have you seen the way he draws up his charts?"

"What's wrong with it?"

"His charts? Haven't you seen his charts? He'll do anything for money."

"Oh, not anything, Olaf."

"Where is he?"

"I last saw him over there." Jerry pointed through the cloudy semi-darkness.

"He's lucky I'll still speak to him." Olaf squiggled off. Jerry leaned against the palm-reading machine, watching him. The Swedish girl came up.

"I don't know *how* long we'll be," she said. "Shades still has many tokens left. He has been winning."

"We could go and smoke something at a *schwartzer* club I know where we wouldn't be unwelcome and the drumming is great. Only if I want to play tonight, it won't help by the time I get to the Friendly Bum."

"You mean marijuana, I think. I don't want to do that. Are you a 'junkie'?"

"Not generally speaking. I leave that up to my brother. We could just go there."

"Where is it?"

"Ladbroke Grove."

"That's far."

"Not that far—only just out of the Area. The other side of no man's land."

"What did you say?"

"Nothing." He glanced over to where Shades was banging a machine. The TILT sign flashed on.

"Fixed!" wept Shades. "Fixed!"

A very cool negro attendant in a white suit glided into sight. He was smiling. "What's the matter, sonny?"

"This table is fixed!"

"Don't be childish. What else you expect?"

Shades appeared to be glowering behind his tired sunglasses. He shrugged rapidly several times. The negro put his head on one side and grinned, waiting.

"You put the odds pretty high in your favour," snarled Shades.

"It's what you got to do, man. Any man's got to do something like that these days, you know. Eh?"

"This whole damned country's crooked."

"You just discovering that, my friend? Oh dear, oh dear."

"It's always been crooked. Sanctimonious crooks."

"Oh, no. They're pretty straightforward these days.

They can afford to be—or thought they could..."

Jerry looked on, amused, as the two ex-patriots talked their cheap philosophy.

Shades shrugged once and turned away. The negro strode off, proud of himself.

Shades's little girl friend trotted across the floor and joined him. He put an arm around her and steered her towards Jerry and the Swedish girl.

"Let's go, Jerry."

"All right."

They spent the last of Jerry's tokens on coffee and pills and set off for the Friendly Bum in Villiers Street, which ran off Trafalgar Square alongside Charing Cross Station, elbowing through the gay night life of the city.

Dragsters, m & f, thronged the Friendly Bum, which was as packed with people as it was with beat, and it was filled to capacity with both. Behind the spotlights, which were turned on the audience, a group could just be made out. A vast amplifier formed the back of the low stage, and a beautiful blend of Hammond organ, pianotron, drums, bass, rhythm and lead guitar, and alto and baritone saxophones, swam out of it, playing "Symphony Sid" with a slow, fugal feeling.

On the low ceiling revolved an old-fashioned dancehall globe made of faceted glass. The lights caught the green, the red, the violet, the gold, the silver and the orange. Light struck it from all directions and was reflected back again so that the photons fairly flew in the Friendly Bum.

They squeezed through a crowd that was all one

mass from which heads and limbs seemed to protrude at random. It was almost unbearably hot.

On the left of the stage was a bar. On the right was a coffee counter. Both were busy. Leaning against the bars were West Indians, elegant in Harlem styles like chorus boys from *Porgy and Bess*. They almost all had thin moustaches and contemptuous looks mainly reserved for the other, less well-dressed West Indians who clapped their hands to every beat but the one the drummer was using.

As they reached the coffee bar on their way to a door behind it marked PRIVATE, Jerry recognised one of the blacks as a musician he had once played with. It was 'Uncle' Willie Stevens, who played flute and tenor and had once done vocals with a since disbanded group called The Allcomers. The group had become popular when it was playing at the Friendly Bum, and the news had spread, until the place had been filled with nothing but groupies and journalists.

"Hello, Uncle."

"Hi, Jerry." Stevens's expression didn't change as he extended a large hand and let Jerry shake it. "What's been happening?"

"This and that. Are you working?"

"Convincing that National Assistance is working. They're getting tougher and tougher every day. They threatened to send me back last week. I said if the NA was more obliging in Birmingham, I'd go back."

"So no scene."

"Oh, there's a good scene, but it's not my scene. You playing here tonight?"

"I hope so."

"I'll be listening."

Jerry walked through the door marked PRIVATE. Shades and the two girls were already in the back room. Shades was getting into his frilly uniform. The other members of the group he played with had theirs on. The guitarists were tuning up. Jerry borrowed the lead guitar, a beautifully made piece of solid polypropylene plastic studded with semi-precious gems with a silver tremolo arm and amplification controls of amethyst. He struck a swift, simple progression of A minor, F, D7 and C. "Nice," he said, handing back the box. "Shades said I could sit in."

"Suits me," said the lead guitar, "so long as you don't want paying."

"I'll wait a couple of numbers until I've heard the group."

"Okay."

"Symphony Sid" was just finishing. Shades and the group went out as the previous group came in. The sixteen-year-old left with Shades. The Swedish girl stayed behind with Jerry. The group who'd just come off were sweating and pleased.

"Let's see if the bar is within arm's reach," Jerry said.

They were lucky. As Shades's group took off on a Lennon/McCartney standard, "It Won't Be Long"—not one of their best—Jerry and the Swede found space at the bar. She was drinking Beaujolais with crème de menthe chasers because she liked the colours. He had a Pernod for old times' sake. He didn't like Pernod, but he'd always drunk it at the Friendly Bum.

"*Every day we'll be happy I know, now that I know that you won't leave me no more*," merrily sang the lead guitar, warming up for the take-off into improvisation. He had a high voice that never missed a quaver. It provided excellent counterpoint for the throbbing organ.

The mass seemed to bubble like a cauldron in time to the music as the clients danced.

Smoothly, the group went straight into "Make It", an instrumental with the pianotron featured. Shades was playing better than Jerry remembered. He and the Swede got up and joined the dancers. The sense of being part of the mass was a delicious feeling. He and the girl and the others around them seemed fused together with a total absence of individual identity.

"Make It" made it, and Shades shouted into his mike, "Jerry!"

Jerry left the floor, crossed the spots, and stood on the stage. The lead guitarist handed him his instrument and went towards the bar with a grin. Jerry played a few chords to get the feel of the amplifier and led off with one of his favourites—another Lennon/McCartney number, "I'm a Loser".

"*I'm a loser and I'm not what I appear to be*," he sang.

As he sang, he saw Miss Brunner come down the steps into the Friendly Bum and look around. She probably couldn't see him behind the lights. She took a step towards the bubbling crowd and then hesitated. Jerry Cornelius forgot her as he began the instrumental improvisation.

Behind him Shades changed from 4/4 to 6/8, but Jerry kept on a 4/4 beat and liked it. The thing began to move now.

Jerry watched the time, careful not to let it go on too long, but close to every stopping point something new occurred to him, and the clients seemed to be enjoying themselves. The piece lasted a good half-hour and left Jerry tired.

"Great," said Shades—praise indeed—as Jerry climbed through the spots and took the lead guitarist's place at the bar. The Swedish girl had been absorbed into the crowd long since.

"Hello, Miss Brunner." A Pernod would suit him now; long and cool, with lots of ice. He ordered one. She paid for it at the same time as she paid for her Scotch.

"What were you playing up there?"

"Instrument or number?"

"Instrument."

"Guitar."

"I haven't got a very good ear. When did you leave Sunnydales?"

"This afternoon. Don't pay them a day past it."

"I won't. I had a hard time getting you there, what with one thing and another. I should think I saved your life."

"Very kind of you. Thanks. I am grateful. I think that does it, don't you?"

"Strictly speaking, yes. Mind you, your thanks could take a more positive form."

"It could."

"Are you still worried about killing your sister?"

"Naturally. And that does that one. What have you been doing with yourself?"

"I advertised for a replacement for Dimitri. I've got a girl on trial. I've got to meet her later. I've been checking some data on the new Burroughs-Wellcome. I didn't realise you were the Cornelius who'd published that unified-field theory."

"You've been digging, Miss Brunner."

"I have."

Overhead the glass ball revolved, and the light struck Miss Brunner's face until it became a flashing assortment of colours. It seemed to offer a clue to her real identity, the total identity that Cornelius had been worrying about since they had talked earlier in Mr Smiles's house at Blackheath. He saw her now as a prism, and through the prism Miss Brunner ceased to be a woman at that moment. She was speaking.

"Weren't you awarded a Nobel Prize for that?"

"A noble price? Ah, I'm just an amateur. It wasn't fair to take it."

"It was your chance of immortality—you may never have another."

Around them mingled sound, light and flesh.

"There is a flaw, you know," she said, "in quite an early equation."

"You spotted it. Are you going to shop me?"

"It could mean immortality for me."

"I think you already have that, Miss Brunner."

"Kind of you to say so. What makes you think it?"

Jerry wondered if he were in any danger. Not at this stage, he decided. "Far better mathematicians than you have checked it and found nothing wrong. You couldn't possibly know—not unless…"

Miss Brunner smiled and sipped her Scotch.

"Unless you had direct experience of what I suggest in my theory, Miss Brunner—unless you *know* better."

"Ah—you are a clever one, Mr Cornelius."

"Where's all this leading to?"

"Nowhere. Shall we go somewhere quieter?"

"I like it here."

"Is there somewhere quieter you like to go?"

"There's the Chicken Fry in Tottenham Court Road."

"Every item on the menu guaranteed vitamin-free. I know the place."

"You are a clever one, Miss Brunner."

As they left, the performers began to destroy their instruments.

"Miss Brunner," he said, leaning over his chicken and fries, "if I hadn't been through my theological phase, I'd be identifying you as first suspect for Mephistophelis."

"I haven't got a pointed beard. Not with me."

"I can't fit you in with *Homo sapiens*."

"I don't fit in easily anywhere." She stabbed herself a forkful of chips.

Jerry leaned behind him and fed tokens into the jukebox. He pressed buttons at random.

"You're sure you're barking up the right tree?" She spoke with her mouth full.

"For a long time I haven't been sure of anything. We'll let the whole thing ride."

"The House of Cornelius still stands," she said. "We didn't get a chance to set it on fire. Does that bother you?"

"Not much. Frank is currently the random factor."

"I have it on good authority that he's in Lapland. To be more accurate, he is two days' trek north-west of Kvikjokk—a small village well beyond Kiruna. Are you that interested?"

"No." He sat back and listened to the music.

"Frank is living in a disused meteorological post in the wilds. We could get there by helicopter."

"I've got a helicopter. And a plane."

"You've got a lot of things like that."

"Anticipation. I still want to get my hands on a private oil well and a small refinery. Then I'm set up."

"You look ahead."

"I look around. Ahead's here already."

"Frank, I suspect, not only has the microfilm your father left. He also has the Newman manuscript."

"Telepathic powers?"

"No—an educated guess. A lot of people have heard that Newman wrote a book after he came down from that capsule last year and before he committed suicide. I've heard that a rep of Newman's widow was looking for Frank. I found the rep, but all he'd tell me was where Frank would be."

"Newman was rubbed out by Security, I thought. Indirect suicide, I suppose. Do you know what was in the book?"

"Some say the complete objective truth about the nature of humanity. Some say a lot of crackpot ideas. It must be one of those books."

"I'd like to read it nonetheless."

"I thought you might. Then we have something in common again?"

"Yes. Where did you say he was near?"

"Kvikjokk—close to Jokmokk."

"Get away with you." Jerry rose. "I'll need some good maps."

"I suppose so. Can we make it by helicopter?"

"That depends. I've got one of those new Vickers long-range copters and fuel caches all across Europe, but the last one's near Uppsala. Lapland's a long way from Uppsala. We could probably get there but not back."

"We'll *float* back, Mr Cornelius, if what I suspect is there."

"What do you suspect?"

"Ah, well—I'm not sure. I've just got a feeling."

"You and your feelings."

"They've never done you any harm."

"They'd better not, Miss Brunner."

"It would be a good thing to start tomorrow morning," she said. "How do you feel?"

"I've been in the hospital, remember. I've made up a lot of ground. I'll last."

"Got you," she said. She picked up her handbag, and they walked out into Tottenham Court Road. "I've got to meet this new girl of mine," she told him. "Her name's Jenny Lumley. She was doing sociology at Bristol until they closed the university down last summer."

"Where are you meeting her?"

"The Blackfriars Ring."

"The wrestling stadium. What's she doing there?"

"She likes wrestling."

They walked to Shaftesbury Avenue, where he got his car out of the garage and drove her to the Blackfriars Ring. It was a big, modern building, specially built for wrestling bouts. Outside, and somewhat jerkily, two neon wrestlers played out a throw time and time again.

There was a big foyer lined with framed pictures of men and women wrestlers. Some of the women even looked nice, but Jerry didn't fancy any of the men. There were three box offices—one on either side and one in the centre. From loudspeakers above them came the relayed roar of the crowd.

Miss Brunner went to the central desk and spoke to the cute little man there. "Miss Brunner—you should have two tickets reserved for me. Our friend's already inside."

He sorted through a small pile of buff envelopes printed with the name of the promoter-owners of the Blackfriars Ring.

"Here we are, dear. Good seats—C705 and 7. You'd better hurry up—the main bout's beginning in a couple of minutes."

"Have you ever seen one of these, Mr Cornelius?" she asked as they walked up the plush stairs.

"Not my speed. I've seen a little on TV."

"Nothing like the real thing."

They went up three flights and walked round the gallery until they came to a door marked 700. The doors must have been well soundproofed, because when they opened them the noise that hit them was loud, an ululating roar. The smell matched the sound. Sweat, perfume and aftershave.

The stadium was about the same size as the Albert Hall, with banks and banks of seats rising into semi-darkness. It was packed. Below, as they looked for their seats, they could see two women throwing each other around by their long hair. There were two referees—one in a chair suspended over the ring and one outside the ring, with his face close to the canvas.

The people in the seats were not all intent on the bout. Many had rid themselves of most of their clothes, and some were entertaining the surrounding fellow spectators better than the pair in the ring.

Looking up and behind him, Jerry noted that there were a lot of children in the cheaper seats. They *were* watching the wrestling. Amplifiers above the banks of seats picked up the groans and shouts of the two contestants as they twisted about in a way Jerry could admire but not understand.

Here and there people were masturbating. "Quite like the old Roman arena, isn't it?" said Miss Brunner with a grin. "I sometimes think that masturbation is the only sincere form of sexual expression left to the unadventurous, poor souls."

"Well, at least they don't bother anyone."

"I think I can see Jenny. You'll like her. She's from the West Country originally—Taunton. She's got those lovely dark West Country looks. Don't they? I'm not so sure. Yes, it is Jenny. And *you* can talk, Mr Cornelius."

"What are you getting at?" They had to push past four or five people to reach their seats. The people didn't get up.

"Oh, nothing. Hello, Jenny, my sweet. This is Mr Cornelius, an old associate of mine."

Jenny looked up with a cocky smile. "Hello, Mr Cornelius." She had long black hair, as fine as Jerry's; a simple shift dress of dark pink; and a red-trimmed leather jacket. She had large dark eyes and was as Miss Brunner had described her. She was also, it seemed, pretty tall. "You got here just in time."

"So we were told." Jerry sat down next to her, and Miss Brunner sat on the other side. Jerry was a sucker for girls like Jenny. When it came down to it, he thought, enjoying her being so close to him, they were the only kind he could go for. There just weren't enough to go round. He smiled to himself. It might be an idea to get her away from Miss Brunner.

It was intermission, and everybody was relaxing as the MC shouted something about the winner and the contestants in forthcoming bouts.

"Who was it said that sex was just two people trying to occupy the same body?" Jenny got a bag of butterscotch from her pocket and handed it round. Jerry liked butterscotch best. "I'm sure I read it—I don't think anyone said it to me. I think it applies just as much to wrestling, don't you, Miss Brunner?"

Miss Brunner's right cheek bulged as she bit her butterscotch.

"I've never thought about it, dear."

"I don't just enjoy the social side of wrestling," she said. "I like the violence and everything too."

Jerry just sat and ogled her while her head was turned to Miss Brunner. Miss Brunner noticed him and raised her eyebrows. Jenny's head shot round and she looked at Jerry, caught him half off guard, and gave him a cheerful wink. Jerry groaned silently. It was too much. It wasn't as if he often met a girl like this. He wished he hadn't come.

The rather garbled voice of the MC came through the amplifiers.

"And now, ladies and gentlemen, the main contest of the evening. In a specially prepared ring we bring you six of our biggest stars in an all-out tag match. Just to add excitement and extra thrills to the contest, we are filling the ring with thick whitewash, as you can see—" Having brought in a special tray that occupied the whole of the inside area of the ring, attendants were now pumping in the thick whitewash.

"Only one of the best can win this match, ladies and gentlemen. And who is to be the best of the six best? Let me read out the names."

The MC now flourished a large piece of paper.

"Doc Gorilla!"

Cheers from supporters.

"Lolita del Starr!"

Enthusiastic shouts.

"Tony Valentine!"

The volume rose…

"Cheetah Gerber!"

… and rose…

"The Masked Crusher!"

… and rose…

"Ella Speed!"

…and rose. There were screams and cheers and boos and a wild, raving sound that was a combination of all the voices.

Jerry looked up, hearing a strange shrilling noise above him. One of the cables leading from the ceiling to the ring held a ski chair, which was speeding downward. In it sat a heavily built woman in her late twenties. She wore a leopardskin bikini and had nice legs. As the chair reached the ring, she jumped from it lightly and sent up a spray of whitewash. She held her balance in the slippery stuff and grinned and waved at the audience. The chair returned, and Jerry could just see the gallery far up near the roof where another small figure was climbing into the chair. It swished down bearing a gross masked man in black long johns and bowling shoes. He too bounced from chair to ring and waved briefly to the audience before flexing at the ropes. Down came the next—a slim girl with long blonde hair in a white one-piece costume. Jerry wondered how she would get the whitewash out of her hair when the bout was over. While she blew kisses at the audience, the older woman suddenly leaped on her, knocking her flat into the whitewash. The crowd moaned and booed. One of the referees on the ground shouted something, and the older woman surlily helped the younger one up. A huge black-bearded, hairy-chested man—evidently Doc Gorilla—was the next arrival. Then a tall, slim, well-muscled woman arrived. She had a handsome, heavy-boned face and dark hair almost to her waist. Lastly came a broad-shouldered, slim-hipped youngster with very short blond hair and white shorts and boots. He smiled at the audience.

Now the overhead referee was moved out to his position above the ring. Four other referees took their places outside the ring, one on each side.

The match began.

It gave Jerry no kicks, but he watched with some amusement at the whitewash-covered tangle below, at the ecstatic crowd. When Jenny gripped his hand he felt pleased until he saw that Miss Brunner was gripping her other hand.

The young blonde in the white one-piece was having her arm twisted by her old enemy. Probably Lolita del Starr and Cheetah Gerber, Jerry decided. Doc Gorilla, the hairy one, looking like the Old Man of the Sea with his beard covered in whitewash, was in a tie-up with the other girl, Ella Speed, and handsome Tony Valentine. Somewhere out of sight beneath them was the Masked Crusher, who didn't seem to be doing much crushing.

Though he couldn't summon up the same enthusiasm as the rest of the audience, Jerry sat back and relaxed. Soon all the wrestlers were so covered in whitewash that it was impossible from where he sat to recognise who was who.

He shouted in Jenny's ear, "You can't tell the men from the women, can you?"

She seemed to hear and shouted something back, which he missed the first time. She shouted it again. "Not these days, no!"

The match went on, with people dancing about, being bounced on ropes, flying out of the ring, climbing back in again, performing acrobatics and contortions of odd complexity.

As a finale with a twist, Tony Valentine and Ella Speed jumped up and grabbed the overhead referee's legs, hauling him into the ring. Then the ref sped round the ring hurling all the wrestlers out over the ropes. The crowd cheered.

Winners were announced and the ring cleared of its whitewash tray.

"And now, ladies and gentlemen, that famous folk group, whose songs have heartened the oppressed all round the world, will entertain you during the intermission. Ladies and gentlemen—The Reformers!"

The Reformers were clapped into the ring. Two men and a good-looking girl with a pointed, self-indulgent face and fair curls. The two men held Spanish guitars. They began to sing a slow song about out-of-work miners. The audience seemed to be enjoying it as it tidied itself up and bought refreshments from the girls who were now trotting round.

"God, aren't they awful?" said Jenny. "They're *ruining* the song. It's one of Woody Guthrie's, you know—very moving. They've sugared it horribly!"

"Oh, I don't know," said Jerry. "Wasn't the group originally The Thundersounds—one of those rhythm-and-blues groups that had a record at the top a couple of years ago? Social conscience, Jenny, it's a good gimmick."

"It's all wrong."

"You're right, love. When pop stars started getting a social conscience, that was the beginning of the end for the social-conscience business."

She gave him a baffled look.

"Are you being contentious, Jerry?" Miss Brunner leaned across the girl.

"Oh, you know…" he said.

"Would you mind if we left now, Jenny?" said Miss Brunner.

"There's only two more matches, Miss Brunner," said Jenny. "Can't we stay and see them?"

"I'd rather we went home now."

"I was looking forward to the match between Doc Gorilla and Tony Valentine."

"I think we ought to go, Jenny."

Jenny sighed.

"Come along," said Miss Brunner, firmly but kindly.

Jenny rose resignedly. They filed from the arena and walked out of the stadium. Jerry had left his car in the nearby lot. Miss Brunner and Jenny got in the back. Jerry started the car and reversed into the street. "Where now?"

"Holland Park. Quite near you, I think." Miss Brunner sat back. "If you go to Holland Park Avenue, I'll direct you from there."

"Okay."

"If we're leaving first thing in the morning, it would be a good idea if you spent the night at my place," Miss Brunner said after a bit.

"Or you at mine."

"Out of the question; I'm sorry."

"Why? Afraid of the gossip?"

"I've got things to do. All you've got to do is pack a bag and come round. We've got a spare bedroom. You'd be quite safe. It bolts on the inside."

"That sounds comforting."

"You're not joking, are you?" Jenny sounded a little surprised.

"No, love."

They reached Notting Hill and drove along Holland Park Avenue. Miss Brunner told him to turn off to the left, and he did so. Another turning, and they were outside a smart, countrified house.

"Here we are," said Miss Brunner. "What do you think of my suggestion? If you popped round to your place and packed a bag, you could be back in a quarter of an hour and I'd have some coffee for you."

"You can produce better inducements than that. Okay." Jerry was still riding with the tide.

As he drove back to Holland Park Avenue and his own large house, he realised that Miss Brunner had been doing a lot of checking. He knew he hadn't told her where he lived.

He left the car standing in the street and went up to the steel gate in the high wall. He said very quietly, "This is a raid." Responding to the sonic code, the door swung open and closed again as Jerry walked up the overgrown path to the house. Another murmured code opened the front door.

Less than a quarter of an hour later, bearing a large suitcase, he left the house and got into his car, put the case on the seat beside him, and returned to Miss Brunner's house.

He rang the bell, and Jenny let him in. She looked as if she'd been taking some rough mental battering while he'd been away, but it might have been just the different light. She gave him a small nervous smile, and he patted her arm reassuringly. Obviously Miss Brunner wasn't planning to take Jenny with her to Lapland, and when they got back he'd make a strong attempt to take Jenny away from Miss Brunner. Jenny didn't realise it but her knight was already plotting her rescue. He hoped she wanted to be rescued. She'd better.

Miss Brunner sat pouring coffee from a Dunhill Filter finished in electric red. It went with the rest of the room, which was mainly red and grey but pretty featureless—just a long couch and a coffee table.

"How do you like it, Mr Cornelius?"

"I always like it how it comes."

"So you say."

"My helicopter is near Harwich. If we started really early we should be able to drive down without too much trouble."

"That suits me. What time—seven?"

"Seven." He took the cup of coffee, drank it down and handed back the cup. She poured him another expressionlessly and gave it to him. He leaned on the wall—slim, serene and elegant.

Miss Brunner looked him over. He had natural style, she thought. Maybe it had once been studied but it was natural now. Her mouth watered.

"Where's this safe bed?" he asked.

"Upstairs, first one you come to at the top."

"Fine. Want me to give you a knock around six?"

"I don't think that'll be needed. I'm not sure I'll be sleeping."

"It must be chess and it can't be bridge. I can see I'm not necessary."

She looked up at him. "Oh, I wouldn't say that."

When Jerry entered the room, he closed the door behind him, locked it, and pulled the bolt. He still didn't feel quite right. There was a shower in the room, and he used it, got into bed and went to sleep.

He was awake at six, showered again, and dressed. He decided to go down and make himself some coffee if

Miss Brunner and Jenny weren't up yet.

Downstairs he heard a noise in the living room and went in. Miss Brunner, dressed as she'd been the previous night, was lying on the couch with her arms flung back and her legs asprawl. Jerry grinned. The noise he had heard was her breathing, deep and ecstatic. At first he guessed that she was drugged, but there wasn't any evidence around. Then he saw a neatly folded deep pink dress, a red-edged leather jacket and a pair of black tights and pumps. Jenny's clothes. Where was Jenny?

He looked down at Miss Brunner's face and felt funny.

He felt even funnier when the eyes popped open and she stared up at him with a quick but dreamy smile.

"What's the time?"

"Time for you to change while I make the coffee. What happened to Jenny?"

"She won't be coming with us—or maybe…" She swung herself into a sitting position, straightening her skirt. "It doesn't matter. Okay, you make some coffee, then we'll be off."

Jerry looked at Jenny's clothes and frowned. Then he looked at Miss Brunner and frowned again.

"Don't worry, Mr Cornelius."

"I've got a feeling I ought to."

"Just a feeling? Ignore it."

"I've got a feeling I ought to do that too." He went out of the room and found the kitchen. He filled the kettle, let it boil, put coffee into the filter, added the water and put the pot on the stove. He heard Miss Brunner go upstairs.

He sat down on a stool, not so much puzzling over Jenny's disappearance as trying not to. He sighed, feeling cold and rough.

7

"You know what Jung thought, don't you?" Jerry tilted the copter up into the clear winter sky. "He reckoned history went in two-thousand-year cycles and that the current cycle started with Christ."

"Didn't he work flying-saucer sightings into that theory too?"

"I believe he did."

"It was all so fuzzy—all that stuff written ten or more years ago."

"There were a lot of hints."

"There are more now."

"And something to do with the zodiacal signs—that thing of Jung's."

"Yes. According to him, we were entering a cycle of great physical and psychological upheavals."

"That isn't hard to spot."

"Not with the Bomb already developed."

The helicopter was nearing the coast, with Holland as the first stop.

"You think it could be as simple as that—the Bomb as the cause?" Miss Brunner looked down at the land and ahead at the sea.

"It could be, after all," he said. "Why does the Bomb have to be a symptom?"

"I thought we had agreed it was."

"So we had. I'm afraid my memory isn't as good as yours, Miss Brunner."

"I'm not so sure. For the last few weeks I've been having hundreds of déjà-vu experiences. What with your ideas on cyclic time—Major Nye…"

"You've been reading my books?" He was annoyed.

"No. Only about them. I haven't been able to get hold of a copy of anything. Privately printed, were they?"

"More or less."

"Why aren't there any around?"

"They disintegrated."

"Shoddy jobs, then."

"No. Built-in obsolescence."

"I'm not with you."

"I'm not with you; that's more to the point." He was still brooding about Jenny. He felt a pretty useless knight now.

"You're talking like that because you don't understand."

"You should have gone to bed last night; you're getting pretty corny."

"Okay." She shut up.

He felt like crashing the copter into the sea, but he couldn't do it. He was afraid of the sea. It was the idea of the Mother Sea that had put him off Celtic mythology as a boy. If only Brother Louis hadn't brought up the same image, he might still be in the Order.

So Miss Brunner was having déjà-vu hallucinations too. Well, it was that kind of old world, wasn't it?

He realised he was getting morbid, reached over, switched on his radio and put the bead in his ear. The music cheered him up.

Thirty miles north of Amsterdam they landed in a field close to farm buildings. The farmer was not surprised. He came hurrying out with cans of fuel. Jerry and Miss Brunner got out to stretch their legs, and Jerry helped the farmer, whom he paid well, to fill the tanks.

Five miles east of Uppsala they had to land and carry the fuel themselves from a barn to the copter. The snow, deep and crisp and even, got in their shoes, and Miss Brunner shivered.

"You might have warned me, Mr Cornelius."

"I'd forgotten. I've never been this way in winter, you see."

"Elementary geography…"

"Which, apparently, neither of us possesses."

They entered a blizzard after a hundred miles, and Jerry had difficulty controlling the copter. When it was over he said to Miss Brunner, "We can get ourselves killed at this rate. I'm going to put her down. We'll have to find a car or something and continue the journey by land."

"That's foolish. It will take three days at least."

"All right," he said. "But another storm like that one and we walk if necessary."

There was not another bad storm, and the copter performed better than Jerry had expected it to. Miss Brunner read the map, and he followed her precise directions.

Below, black scars winding through the snow showed the main roads. Great frozen rivers and snow-laden forest stretched in all directions. Ahead they could just see a range of old, old mountains. It was perpetual evening at this time of year, and the further north they went, the darker it became. The white lands seemed uninhabited, and Jerry could easily see how the legends of trolls, Jotunheim, and the tragic gods—the dark, cold, bleak legends of the North—had come out of Scandinavia. It made him feel strange, even anachronistic, as if he had gone back in time from his own age to the Ice Age.

It was becoming increasingly difficult to make out what lay beneath them, but Miss Brunner persevered, scanning the ground with night-glasses and continuing her directions. Although the copter was well heated, they were both shivering.

"There are a couple of bottles of Scotch in the back," said Jerry. "Better get one."

She found a bottle of Bell's, unscrewed the cap and handed the bottle to him. He gulped some down and handed it to her. She did the same.

"That's cheered me up," he said.

"We're getting close. Go down. There's a Lapp village marked on this map and I think we just passed it. The station isn't much farther."

The station seemed to be built of rust-red sheets of steel. Jerry wondered how they had got the materials there in the first place. Snow had been cleared round it, and a metal chimney blew black smoke into the air.

In that odd twilight, Jerry landed the copter on the snow and switched off the engine. A door opened, and a man stood there holding a portable electric lamp. It wasn't Frank.

"Good afternoon," Jerry called in Swedish. "Are you alone?"

"Absolutely. You are English by your accent. Were you forced down?"

"No. I understand that my brother was here."

"A man was here yesterday before I arrived. He went towards the mountains on a snowmobile, by the signs. Come in."

He led them into the cabin, closing the triple doors behind him. A stove blazed in the room they entered. Another room led off it.

The little man had a slightly Asiatic cast of face, reminding Jerry, too, of an Apache Indian. He was probably a Lapp. He was dressed in a large, heavy coat that covered him from neck to ankles. It looked like tawny wolfskin. He put the lamp on a deal table and waved towards some straight-backed chairs.

"Sit. I have some soup on the stove." He went to

the range and took a medium-sized iron saucepan off it. He put it on the table. "I am Marek—the local pastor to the Lapps, you know. I had a reindeer team, but the wolverines got one of them yesterday, and I couldn't control the other and had to let it go. I expect a villager will discover it and come and look for me. Meanwhile I am warm here. There are provisions. Luckily, I am allowed a key to the place. I replace the supplies from time to time, and they allow me to use it on such an occasion as this."

"My name is Cornelius," said Jerry. "This is Miss Brunner."

"Not *English* names."

"No. But Marek isn't a Swedish name," Jerry smiled. Miss Brunner looked vexed, unable to understand the conversation.

"You are right, it is not. You know Sweden?"

"Only as far as Umea. I've never been this far north—not in winter at all."

"We must seem strange to someone who sees us only in the summer." Marek reached into a locker over the stove and took out three bowls and a loaf of rye bread. "We are not a summer people—winter is our natural time, though we hate it!"

"I'd never thought of that." Jerry turned to Miss Brunner and told her the basic details of their conversation as Marek poured the soup.

"Ask him where Frank might be going," said Miss Brunner.

"Is he a meteorologist?" Marek asked when Jerry put the question.

"No, though I think he's got some knowledge of it."

"He could be going to Kortafjallet—it's one of the highest mountains near here. There's another station on the summit."

"I can't see him going there. Anywhere else?"

"Well, unless he was going to try to get through the Kungsladen to Norway—it's the pass that runs through these mountains—I can't think. There are no villages in the direction he took."

Jerry told Miss Brunner what Marek had said.

"Why should he want to go to Norway?" she said.

"Why should he want to come *here*?"

"It's remote. He probably knew I was after him, though he thought you were dead. Maybe someone told him otherwise."

"Frank wouldn't come to somewhere as cold as this unless he had a real reason."

"Was he working on anything that would involve his being here?"

"I don't think so." Jerry turned to the pastor again. "How long would you say this man had been here?"

"A week or longer, judging by the low state of the supplies."

"I suppose he left nothing behind him?"

"There was some paper. I used some of it to light the stove, but the rest should be in this bin." The priest reached under the table. "Aren't you going to eat your soup?"

"Yes. Thanks."

When they were sitting down eating, Jerry smoothed out the quarto sheets of paper. The first contained some doodles.

"Frank's in a bad way." Jerry passed it to Miss Brunner.

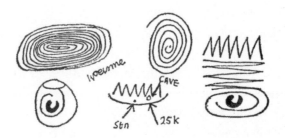

"That's the interesting one." Miss Brunner pointed at the doodle with the lettering. "It gives our position and, I'd guess, his destination. But what's it all about?"

Jerry studied the other three sheets. There were some figures that he couldn't make sense of and more neurotic symbols. There was a pattern there, but he didn't feel like digging too deep. Knowing Frank, he was more disturbed by these doodles than he normally would have been.

"The best way of finding out is to follow him and locate this cave. Maze symbols, womb symbols. It's Frank's signature, without a doubt. He's developed a nice fat persecution complex."

"I'm not sure," said Miss Brunner. "You couldn't blame him, really. After all, we have been persecuting him."

"It's about even, I'd say. I don't feel up to going any

further tonight. Shall we stay here?"

"Yes."

"Do you mind if we spend the night here?" Jerry asked Marek.

"Of course not. It's a strange place for you, no doubt, to celebrate the season."

"The season? What's the date?"

"The twenty-fourth of December."

"Merry Christmas," said Jerry in English.

"Merry Christmas," smiled Marek, also in English. Then he said in Swedish, "You must tell me what things are like in the rest of Europe."

"Pretty good."

"I have read that inflation exists almost everywhere. Your crimes of violence have risen steeply, as have mental disorders, vice…"

"IBM has just perfected a new predictor-computer, using British, Swedish and Italian scientists; all kinds of books and papers are being published full of new observations about the sciences, the arts—even theology. There have never been so many. Transport and communications are better than they ever were…" Jerry shook his head. "Pretty good."

"But what of the spiritual state of Europe? We share most of your problems, you know, other than the economic and political ones—"

"They'll come. Be patient."

"You are very cynical, Herr Cornelius. I am tempted to believe that Ragnarok is almost with us."

"That's an odd thing for a Christian minister to say."

"I am more than that—I am a Scandinavian Lutheran. I have no doubt of the truths inherent in our old pagan mythology. Herr Cornelius, I would very much like to know your real reason for coming here."

"I've told you. We are searching for my brother."

"There is much more than that. I am not an intellectual, but I have an instinct that is generally quite astute. There is at once something *less* and something *more* in both you and your companion. Something—I am not normally guilty of coming to such a stern assumption—something evil."

"There's good and bad in all of us, Herr Marek."

"I see your face—and your eyes. Your eyes look boldly at much that I would fear to look at, but also they seem to hide from things that do not frighten me."

"Could it be that we are ahead of you, Herr Marek?"

"Ahead? In what way?"

"In *time*." Jerry felt unusually angry with the pastor. "These old-fashioned rules no longer apply. Your sort of morality, your sort of thinking, your sort of behaviour—it was powerful in its day. Like the dinosaur. Like the dinosaur it cannot survive in this world. You put values on everything—values…"

"I think I can see a little of what you mean." Marek lost his composure and rubbed his face. "I wonder… is it Satan's turn to rule?"

"Careful, Herr Marek, that's blasphemy. Besides, what you are saying is meaningless nowadays." Jerry's hair had become disarranged as he talked. He brushed it back from the sides of his face.

"Because you want it to be?" Marek turned and walked towards the stove.

"Because it *is*. I am scarcely self-indulgent, Herr Marek—not in present-day terms."

"So you have your own code." Marek sounded almost jeering.

"On the contrary. There is no new morality, Herr Marek—there is no morality. The term is as barren as your grandmother's wrinkled old womb. There *are* no values!"

"There is still one fact we can agree on. Death."

"*Death? Death? Death?*" There were tears in his eyes. "*Why?*"

"Have you decided to start from scratch?" Marek was rising now to Jerry's challenge. Jerry was disconcerted and miserable.

"D—" Jerry paused.

"What's going on?" Miss Brunner stood up. "What are you two quarrelling about?"

"The old bloke's round the twist." Jerry's voice was low.

"Really? Can you ask him where we sleep and if there are any spare blankets?"

Jerry relayed the request.

"Follow me." Marek led them into the adjoining room. There were four bunks, two pairs. He lifted the mattress off one of the bottom bunks, pulled back a panel and began lifting out blankets. "Enough?"

"Fine," said Jerry.

Jerry took the top bunk, Miss Brunner the bottom, and Marek slept in the bottom bunk opposite them. They all slept fully clothed, wrapped in blankets.

Jerry slept badly and woke in darkness. He looked at his watch and saw that it was 8 a.m. The pastor's bunk was empty. He leaned over and peered down. Miss Brunner was still sleeping. He unwrapped himself and jumped·down.

In the other room, Marek was cooking something on the stove. On the table were an opened tin of herrings and three plates and forks.

"Your brother took most of our provisions, I'm afraid," Marek said as he brought the pot to the table. "Sild and coffee for breakfast. I apologise for my behaviour last night, Herr Cornelius. My own bewilderment got the better of me."

"And mine of me."

"I considered what you had said as best I could. I am now inclined…" Marek got three enamel mugs from the locker and poured coffee into two. "Is Miss Brunner ready for coffee yet?"

"She's still sleeping."

"I am now inclined to believe that there is a certain truth in what you say. I believe in God, Herr Cornelius, and the Bible—yet there are references in the Bible that can be interpreted as indications of this new phase you hint at. Have you read Beesley at all?"

"You shouldn't let yourself be convinced, Herr Marek."

"Don't worry about that. Would it, I wonder, be an

intrusion if I accompanied you on this quest of yours? I believe I know the mountain your brother headed for—there is one with a cave. The Lapps are not very superstitious, Herr Cornelius, but they tend to avoid the cave. I wonder why your brother should be interested in it."

"What do you know about this? I didn't mention it."

"I have a little English. I read the map your brother drew."

"Could you make sense of the rest?"

"It made some sort of sense to my—well, my instincts. I don't know why."

"You can lead us there?"

"I think so. This is hardly the weather…"

"Will it be too dangerous?"

"Not if we take it carefully."

"I'll wake Miss Brunner."

Through the white twilight of the Arctic winter the three people moved. On the higher parts of the ground stood a few silver birches, and on their left was a frozen lake, a wide expanse of flat snow. A little snow drifted in the air, and the clouds above were dense and grey.

A world of perpetual evening which would for six weeks in the year, Jerry knew, become a lush and glorious world of perpetual afternoon when the sun never went below the horizon, where lakes shone and rivers ran, animals moved, trees, rushes, gorse flourished. But now it was a moody, unfriendly landscape. By this time the station was out of sight behind them. It seemed that they were hardly on earth at all, for the grey day stretched in all directions.

They followed Marek on the snowshoes he had found for them. The landscape, silent and still, seemed to impose its own silence on them, for they spoke little as they walked, huddled in their clothes.

At long last the mountains came in sight, and they picked up the faint tracks of Frank's snowmobile winding ahead of them. The mountains were close, but they hadn't seen them until now because of the poor visibility.

Jerry wondered again if Miss Brunner's telling him that Frank had the astronaut's testament was a ruse simply to get him to go along with her. He was not alone in wanting to see what Newman had written. There was something unusual in the way in which he had been silenced, the few wild public statements he had made before that, the fact that he had done more orbits in his capsule than had been originally announced. Would there really be some observation in the manuscript that would clarify the data?

The ground rose and they began to climb awkwardly.

"The cave is quite close," Marek said, his breath streaming out.

Jerry wondered how he could be so sure in this almost featureless country.

The cave mouth had recently been cleared of snow. Just inside they could see the runners of a snowmobile.

Miss Brunner held back.

"I'm not sure that I want to go in. Your brother's insane—"

"But that isn't your reason."

"I've got that 'I've been here before' feeling again."

"Me too. Come on." Jerry entered the dark cave. Its far wall could not be seen. "Frank!"

The echo went on and on.

"It's a big cave," he said. He took his needle gun from his pocket. The others entered behind him.

"I forgot to bring a torch," Marek whispered.

"We'll have to hope for the best, then. It will mean that he won't be able to see us."

The cave was actually a tunnel sloping deeper and deeper into the rock. Clinging together, they stumbled on, uncertain of their footing. Jerry lost all sense of passing time, began to suspect that time had stopped. Events had become so unpredictable and beyond his control that he couldn't think about them. He was losing touch.

The floor of the tunnel and the hands of his companions became the sole reality. He began to suspect that he wasn't moving at all but that the floor was moving under him. He felt mentally and physically numb. Every so often vertigo would come and he would pause, swaying, feeling outward with his foot to find the chasm that was never there. Once or twice he half-fell.

Much later he was able to see the luminous dial of his watch. Four hours had passed. The tunnel seemed to be widening all the time, and he realised that it was

much warmer and deeper and there was a saline smell in his nostrils as if of the sea. His senses began to wake and he heard the echoes of his own footsteps going away into distance. Ahead and below he thought he saw a trace of blue light.

He began to run down the incline, but checked his speed when he found he was going too fast. Now the light was good enough to show him the dim figures of his companions. He waited for them to catch up, and they went on cautiously towards the source of the light.

They came out of the tunnel and were standing on a slab of rock overlooking a gloomy, steamy gallery that stretched out of sight in all directions. Something had made the water slightly luminous, and this was the source of the light—a lake of hot water probably created by some underground hot spring carrying phosphorus. The water boiled and bubbled, and the steam soon soaked them. The floor of the gallery nearest to them was under water, and Jerry could distinguish several objects that looked out of place there. He noted that the rocks on his right led to this beach, and he began to slide down them towards it. The others took his lead.

"I had no idea that there could be a cave system of this size. What do you think caused it?" Miss Brunner was panting.

"Glacier, hot springs carrying corrosives looking for a way out… I've never heard of anything quite like it. Certainly nothing as big." They walked along the slippery, mineral-encrusted rock beside the lake. Jerry pointed. "Boats. Three of them. One of them looks fairly recent."

"These caves must have been known for at least a hundred years." Marek inspected the most dilapidated of the boats. "This is that old." He peered inside. "God save me!"

"What is it?" Jerry looked into the boat. A skeleton looked back at him. "Well, Frank certainly found something. You know, I think I've got an idea about this place. Did you ever hear of the Hollow Earth theory?"

"The last people to place any credence in it were those Nazis," said Miss Brunner, frowning deeply.

"Well, you know what I'm talking about—the idea that there was some sort of entrance in the Arctic to a world inside the earth. I'm not sure, but I think the whole idea was Bulwer-Lytton's—an idea he had in a novel. Didn't Horbiger have the same idea, or was he just for Eternal Ice?"

"You seem to know more about it than I do. But this tie-up with the Nazis is interesting. I hadn't thought of it."

"What tie-up?"

"Oh, I don't know. Anyway, I thought the Nazis believed the world was actually embedded in an infinity of rock—or was that someone else?"

"They gave serious consideration to both. Either theory would have suited them. Radar disproved one, and they could never find the polar opening, though I'm sure they sent at least one expedition."

"They were certainly triers, weren't they?" Miss Brunner said admiringly. Jerry picked up the skull and threw it out over the water.

8

Jerry inspected the most recent-looking boat. "It's seaworthy, I'd say."

"You're not going out over *that*?" Miss Brunner shook her head.

"It must be the way Frank went. What do you think these boats mean? They weren't dragged here for nothing—they've crossed and come back."

"Crossed to what?"

"I thought you wanted to know what Frank was after. This is the way to find out."

"Do you think he believes this Hollow Earth idea?"

"I don't know. Isn't it even possible?"

"It's been disproved hundreds of ways!"

"So have a lot of things."

"Oh, come now, Jerry!"

"What do you think, Herr Marek? Do you want to see if we can cross the hot lake?"

"I am beginning to think that Dante was a naturalistic writer," said the Lapp. "I am glad I decided to come, Herr Cornelius."

"Let's get this boat launched then."

Marek helped him push the rowboat towards the water. It slid along easily. Jerry put one foot in the water and leaped back. "It's hotter than I thought!"

Miss Brunner shrugged and joined them as they steadied the boat.

"You get in first," Jerry told her. Unwillingly, she clambered in. Marek followed her, and Jerry got in last. The boat began to drift out over the phosphorescent water. Jerry unshipped the oars. He began to row through the steaming water, his features, caught in the oscillating radiance, looking like those of a fallen angel.

Soon the wall of the great cavern was obscured, and ahead of them was only vapour and darkness. Jerry began to feel drowsy, but continued to row with long strokes.

"This is like the River of the Dead," Marek said. "And you, Herr Cornelius, are you Charon?"

"I wish I were—it's a steady job, at least."

"I think you see yourself more as Cassandra."

"Cassandra?" Miss Brunner caught a word she understood. "Are you two talking about mythology still?"

"How did you know that was what we'd been talking about?"

"An educated guess."

"You're full of them."

"It's to do with my job," she said.

Marek was in high spirits. He chuckled. "What are you talking about?"

"I'm not sure," Jerry replied.

Marek chuckled again. "You two—you are an ambivalent pair."

"I wish you were wrong, Herr Marek."

Miss Brunner pointed ahead. "There is another shore—can you make anything out?"

He turned. The shore ahead seemed studded with regularly spaced and perfect cubes, some about two feet high and others ten feet high.

"Could that be a natural formation, Herr Cornelius?"

"I don't think so. In this light you can't even see what they're made of."

As they rowed nearer, they could see that some of the cubes were not on the shore at all but partially immersed in water. Jerry paused by one and reached out to touch it. "Concrete."

"Impossible!" Marek seemed delighted.

"You can't say that until we know more about this place." The bottom of the boat scraped the shore and they got out, hauling the boat after them.

They were surrounded by the black outlines of the concrete cubes. They approached the nearest.

"It's a bloody bunker!" Jerry entered it. There was a light switch inside the door, but it didn't work when Jerry tried it. He couldn't see anything of the interior. He went outside and walked around the bunker until he came to the machine-gun slit. The gun was still there, pointing out over the underground lake. He grasped the gun and took his hand away covered in gritty rust. "They're not new. What is it—some abandoned Swedish project to guard against Russian attacks? All the roads into Finland have posts like these, haven't they, Herr Marek?"

"They have. But this is Lappish land—the government would need Lapp permission. They are very particular about the rights of the Lapps in Sweden, Herr Cornelius. I think the Lapps would have known about it."

"Not if there were security reasons. This place would be perfect as an H-bomb shelter. I wonder…"

Miss Brunner called through the gloom. "Mr Cornelius, I don't think this was a Swedish project."

They went over to where she stood beside a light armoured car. The paint had partially peeled off it, but the remains of a swastika could be seen.

"A German project. But the Swedish government was neutral during the war, and this couldn't have been built in complete secrecy." He translated for Marek.

"Maybe just one or two people in the government knew and covered up," Marek suggested. "The Swedes were not always Anglophiles."

"But why should they build it?"

Through the regular rows of bunkers they moved— living quarters, offices, radio posts, a complete military village hundreds of feet below ground. Abandoned.

"That expedition of Hitler's may not have found the land at the earth's core," Miss Brunner was saying, "but evidently they thought this place worth using. I wonder what purpose they had for it."

"Perhaps none at all. For a people who burbled all the time about purpose they were great ones for forgetting their reasons for doing things."

The rock began to slope upward, and the light from the phosphorescent sea began to fade behind them.

"Those Nazis were born out of their time." Jerry led the way. Though the blue light had faded, there was still light of a new quality which seemed almost like daylight. Larger buildings came into sight on the crest of the slope, and Jerry, looking upward into the distance, saw tiny rays of light like stars in a black sky. "I think that's the open air beyond the roof. I think this cavern is only partially natural and the rest was hollowed out. Fabulous engineering."

The larger buildings had probably been the private quarters of officers. Behind them they could just distinguish a long series of structures unlike any of the rest, some sort of scaffolding bearing heavier objects. "Gun emplacements, could they be?" Miss Brunner asked.

"That's probably it."

"Your brother does not seem to be here after all." Marek looked about him.

"He must be. How did he know of this place, though?"

"Frank got around," Miss Brunner pointed out. "He had all sorts of acquaintances. Even I had heard rumours about the entrance to the underground world. This is what started them, I'd guess."

"Why should he come here? It's lonely, disturbing. Frank never liked being lonely or disturbed."

"Jerry, I am now not lonely and I am relaxed. Glad you could make it." On the roof of one of the buildings Frank stood giggling, his needle gun pointing in their general direction.

"Show-off!" Jerry dived straight into the entrance of the building before Frank could shoot. He got his own gun out.

Frank yelled from the roof, "Come out, Jerry, or I'll shoot your friends."

"Shoot them, then."

"Please come out, Jerry. I've been thinking what to do. I'm going to stitch your balls to your thighs. How about it?"

"Who told you I had any?"

"Please come out, Jerry."

"You're a sadist, Frank—I just realised it."

"One of many pleasures. Please come out, Jerry."

"What are you looking for here? Steamy, uterine seas, warm caves. Revealing, Frank."

"You're so common."

"I am indeed."

"Please, please come out, Jerry."

"You're frustrated, Frank, that's all that's wrong with you."

He heard footsteps scramble on the roof, and a hatch opened above him. He fired up as Frank fired down. "This is ridiculous," he said as they repressured. They had both missed. "Do you really want to kill me, Frank?"

"I thought I *had*, Jerry. I don't know."

"You're all the family I have left now, Frank." He laughed, fired and missed again.

"Whose fault was it that Catherine died?" Frank asked as he also missed. "Yours or mine?"

"We're all victims of circumstance." Jerry fired and missed. He had a lot of needles left.

"Yours or mine?"

"Fault, Frank? Blame?"

"Don't you feel guilty, Jerry?" Frank missed.

"On and off, you know."

"There you are, then! Missed!" Both statements were triumphant. "And what about Mum?"

"Missed!"

"Missed!"

"Missed!"

"Jerry."

"What is this place, Frank? How did you find it?"

"It was on Father's microfilm. The one your friends were looking for. Come to think of it, they tortured me, didn't they?"

"I believe so. But what has it got to do with the European economic situation?"

"It would take someone who knew about those things to say. I can't."

"Have you got the Newman manuscript with you?"

"Yes. Missed!"

"Can I see it?"

"You'd laugh if you did. It would suit you down to the ground."

"It's interesting, is it? Missed."

"Oh yes—aaah!"

"Got you!"

Frank's feet stumbled away over Jerry's head. Jerry

ran out of the building and bumped into Miss Brunner and Marek. He paused and then ran round the building.

Frank was limping down towards the shore.

They ran after him.

Frank ducked behind a bunker, and they lost sight of him.

"Look here," said Miss Brunner firmly, taking a .22 from her bag, "we're not going to lose him again."

"I wounded him. We'll find him." They searched among the bunkers, emerging on the shore.

"There's your brother." Marek pointed. He didn't understand the game, but he was joining in enthusiastically.

Jerry and Miss Brunner fired together as Frank tried to push his boat out over the steaming lake. He turned, howled, and fell with a splash. He screamed, thrashing in the boiling water.

He was dead by the time they reached him and dragged him out. "Done to a turn," said Jerry. "For the time being."

There was a briefcase in the bottom of the boat. Miss Brunner covered Jerry with her gun as she stooped and picked it up. Resting it on her knee, she opened it with one hand and reached in. She came out with a microfilm spool and put it in her pocket. She put her gun back in her bag and handed him the briefcase. There was a thick cardboard file containing a typescript. In Frank's handwriting were the words *The Testament of S. Newman, Colonel, USAF, Astronaut.* Jerry flicked off the rubber bands holding the manuscript together. He sat down on the damp rock and opened the file and began to read:

ha ha ha ha ha ha ha ha ha ha ha ha ha ha ha ha ha ha ha
ha ha ha ha ha ha ha ha ha ha ha ha ha ha ha ha ha ha ha
ha ha ha ha ha ha ha ha ha ha ha ha ha ha ha ha ha ha ha
ha ha ha ha ha ha ha ha ha ha ha ha ha ha ha ha ha ha ha
ha ha ha ha ha ha ha ha ha ha ha ha ha ha ha ha ha ha ha
ha ha ha ha ha ha ha ha ha ha ha ha ha ha ha ha ha ha ha
ha ha ha ha ha ha ha ha ha ha ha ha ha ha ha ha ha ha ha
ha ha ha ha ha ha ha ha ha ha ha ha ha ha ha ha ha ha ha
ha ha ha ha ha ha ha ha ha ha ha ha ha ha ha ha ha ha ha
ha ha ha ha ha ha ha ha ha ha ha ha ha ha ha ha ha ha ha
ha ha ha ha ha ha ha ha ha ha ha ha ha ha ha ha ha ha ha
ha ha ha ha ha ha ha ha ha ha ha ha ha ha ha ha ha ha ha
ha ha ha ha ha ha ha ha ha ha ha ha ha ha ha ha ha ha ha
ha ha ha ha ha ha ha ha ha ha ha ha ha ha ha ha ha ha ha
ha ha ha ha ha ha ha ha ha ha ha ha ha ha ha ha ha ha ha
ha ha ha ha ha ha ha ha ha ha ha ha ha ha ha ha ha ha ha
ha ha ha ha ha ha ha ha ha ha ha ha ha ha ha ha ha ha ha
ha ha ha ha ha ha ha ha ha ha ha ha ha ha ha ha ha ha ha
ha ha ha ha ha ha ha ha ha ha ha ha ha ha ha ha ha ha ha
ha ha ha ha ha ha ha ha ha ha ha ha ha ha ha ha ha ha ha
ha ha ha ha ha ha ha ha ha ha ha ha ha ha ha ha ha ha ha
ha ha ha ha ha ha ha ha ha ha ha ha ha ha ha ha ha ha ha
ha ha ha ha ha ha ha ha ha ha ha ha ha ha ha ha ha ha ha
ha ha ha ha ha ha ha ha ha ha ha ha ha ha ha ha ha ha ha
ha ha ha ha ha ha ha ha ha ha ha ha ha ha ha ha ha ha ha
ha ha ha ha ha ha ha ha ha ha ha ha ha ha ha ha ha ha ha
ha ha ha ha ha ha ha ha ha ha ha ha ha ha ha ha ha ha ha
ha ha ha ha ha ha ha ha ha ha ha ha ha ha ha ha ha ha ha
ha ha ha ha ha ha ha ha ha ha ha ha ha ha ha ha ha ha ha

Not a variation on 203 neatly numbered pages of manuscript. Jerry sighed and tossed the book into the water.

PHASE

3

9

He rowed away, leaving Marek and Miss Brunner standing close together on the shore. He was very tired, and he had a long trip ahead of him.

Halfway up the sloping cavern, he lay down to sleep. When he woke up, he climbed on until he reached the cave's mouth. The cold did not bother him as he inspected Frank's snowmobile.

It seemed easy to operate, and the grey tracks it had made coming here were not completely obliterated by snow.

Sad and scared, he followed the tracks back to the station. He sighed deeply all the way, and a few tears even wetted his big black eyes when he stopped the sleigh by the rust-red meteorological post. He went in and opened a tin of herring. The stove had gone out, but the hut was still warmer than it was outside. He ate the herring and went to fetch his bottle from the copter. He sat in the pilot's seat drinking whisky and trying to warm up the engine. He had finished the Scotch by the time it caught. He slid the door open and tossed the bottle out. The copter was a good one. There was probably enough fuel left to get him to one of the Baltic ports. Before he took off, he rummaged in the back and found his passport. There were only a few days to go before it expired.

He dumped the copter outside Lumea and was able to buy a ticket on a cargo ship leaving that night. He convinced the officials that someone must have forgotten to stamp his entry visa in his passport and headed for Southampton, via Hamburg.

In London he opened his town house. The hotel-sized building on Holland Park Avenue stood well back from the street and was surrounded by a high wall topped with electrified spikes.

It was time, he decided, for a spot of exterior meditation. He would get a big party going and lose himself in it. With luck it would help him to work a few things out.

But first he filled himself with sleeping pills and took to his bed to sleep a dreamless sleep for three days and nights. When he woke his energy was low and people were even more urgently needed.

After his bath, he dressed in a high-collared white Bastille-style linen shirt, a black terylene cravat, black suède trousers and black doeskin jacket. From a wardrobe containing some fifteen of them, he took a black, double-breasted car coat and laid it on the chest near the window. He pulled on a pair of black boots with low cuban heels. He studied his pale features in the mirror that covered the far wall, brushed his hair and was satisfied. He was feeling very hungry and rather weak. He picked up the coat, took a new pair of gloves from the chest, and left the dressing room. There were actually two dressing rooms, one containing clothes he would probably never bother to wear.

The house was mid-Victorian, with six floors and two very large main rooms on each floor. Every room was sparsely furnished and gave the impression that the occupant was in the process of moving either in or out.

Jerry walked down the wide stairs until he reached the basement, where the kitchens were. Although they shone with mechanical equipment, the kitchens had hardly been used. Great cupboards were filled with canned and dehydrated food. The cellars below, apart from containing a vast selection of wines and spirits which he never drank, also contained a commercial cold-storage room filled with a mixed herd of carcasses. The whole collection, here and below, made Jerry feel sick when he thought about it. He mixed himself a pot of instant coffee and ate a packet of chocolate digestives.

There were two cars in the garage behind the house. One was a little Toyota mini-sports that the Japanese had just started to put on the market. The other was the oldest thing Jerry owned—the three-ton supercharged 1936

Duesenberg limousine. Custom-built for a successful Midwestern police chief, it had bulletproof glass and steel shutters operated by the push-button window control and automatic lubrication every seventy-five miles and did ninety in second gear. Jerry normally liked plenty of bonnet in front of him when he drove. His other car, the Phantom, was back in the Shaftesbury Avenue garage. His own garage was large enough to house several double-decker buses, and most of it was taken up by drums of fuel. There was also a small petrol reservoir below.

The door slid out of the ground and closed behind him as he drove the Toyota down the asphalt drive into Holland Park Hill, turned left towards Kensington High Street and had a fairly clear drive until he reached the main street.

He played the radio and relaxed in the great solid stream of traffic as it flowed slowly along. Within an hour and a half he had parked the Toyota in his reserved space in the Piccadilly Sky Garage and breathed the rich air of the centre with pleasure. He never felt really comfortable unless he had at least fifteen miles of built-up area on all sides; and here he was happiest, walking towards Leicester Square and the Blue Boar Tavern for a quick cocktail. It wasn't natural, he felt, for a man to have to live any other way.

In times of change, the Blue Boar did not change. The blue neon sign still glimmered outside, the plastic trees on the way down to the cocktail bar still twittered with artificial birdsong, the plastic coat-of-arms still adorned the leatherette-upholstered walls, and the lighting was still low. It was quiet and pleasantly vulgar, and the cocktails were inexpensive.

A small, pretty, dark-haired girl brought Jerry a Woomera Special—milder than the name implied: bourbon with ginger ale. A couple were sitting in the corner, and they paid little attention to Jerry or each other. Once or twice the man asked an abrupt question in German and was answered abruptly. Jerry could rarely speak German.

Leaving the Blue Boar, he went into the Beat City showrooms round the corner to see if his guitar was ready. He had ordered it after his return from Angkor.

The man took him into the basement to see it. It had an oval belly and a 24-fret neck. The strings went up to the top of the neck into a small transistorised sensitiser which automatically kept them in tune. Six pick-ups were ranged between the bridge and the neck, and there was a control for each one, with a tremolo switch and echo play and fuzz buttons. It was one of the best pieces of musical engineering Jerry had seen. The cost was £4,200 plus £1,400 tax. They plugged it into their amplifier so he could test it. It was beautiful, sound as a bell. He gave them a cheque and took it with him.

In a Welbeck Street coffee bar Jerry put in his junk order, buying The Man's entire stock. "If your regulars are put out," he told The Man, "tell them my address and tell them it's free."

At beat clubs, at Emmett's, at bars, in bookshops and boutiques, hairdressers, grills and record shops, Jerry toured and spread the word that an open party was about to start at his Holland Park house.

When he got back to the house, carrying his heavy guitar in its flat case, he was just in time to let in the first truckload of food from the catering firm that had agreed to supply the party with almost everything it would need.

As the white-coated men began to lay the stuff out, Jerry locked the doors leading down to the basement. They were steel, eight inches thick, and would open only to a specific vocal command from him.

On the ground floor, the two rooms could be opened out into one. The only furniture was cushions scattered about on the carpet and a large stereo tele-radiogram-tape-recorder combination. Ten-inch spools of tape were ready, and Jerry switched them on to test them. They relayed music through speakers everywhere in the house.

He began to feel depressed.

He opened the guitar case and took out the instrument. He plugged in the lead and plugged the other end into the combination's amplifier, switching off the tape.

He played a brief E-flat progression, trying out a simple tune based on Rufus Thomas's "All Night Worker". It didn't come out properly. He adjusted the pick-ups and tone controls and tried again, this time in B flat. It had nothing in it. He sighed.

He tried out a number of other basic progressions. Nothing was wrong with the guitar, but there was something wrong with him.

He put the guitar away, switched on the tapes again, and went upstairs to change.

· · · · ·

The Man and a couple of friends were the first arrivals. "I thought I'd avail myself of the facilities," said The Man, taking off his heavy raincoat. He wore a high-collared green corduroy jacket and Hamlet tights. He looked a wow.

The flood was on, and half-suspicious guests got the mood of the place before they let themselves relax. There were Turkish and Persian lesbians with huge houri eyes like those of sad, neutered cats; French tailors, German musicians; Jewish martyrs; a fire-eater from Suffolk; a barber-shop quartet from Britain's remaining American base—the Columbia Club, in Lancaster Gate; two fat prudes; Hans Smith of Hampstead, Last of the Left-Wing Intellectuals—the Microfilm Mind; Shades; fourteen dealers in the same antique from Portobello Road, their faces sagging under the weight of their own self-deception; a jobless Polish french-polisher brought by one of the dealers; a pop group called the Deep Fix; a pop group called Les Coques Sucrés; a tall negro; a hunchbacked veterinarian named Marcus; the Swedish girl and a juicy youngster; three journalists, who had just finished spending their golden handshakes; Little Miss Dazzle, whom one of them had discovered in El Vino's looking for Mr Crookshank; an Irishman called Poodles; the literary editor of the *Oxford Mail* and his sister; twenty-seven members of the Special Branch; a heterosexual; two small children; the late great Charlie Parker, just in from Mexico under his alias Alan Bird—he had been cleaning up for years; a morose psychiatrist from Regent's Park named Harper; a great many physicists, astrologers, geographers, mathematicians, astronomers, chemists, biologists, musicians, monks from disbanded monasteries, warlocks, out-of-work whores, students, Greeks, solicitors; a self-pitying albino; an architect; most of the pupils from the local comprehensive school, who had heard the noise and come in; most of their teachers; Jerry's mum; a market gardener; less than one New Zealander; two hundred Hungarians who had Chosen Freedom and the chance to make a fast buck; a sewing-machine salesman; the mothers of twelve of the children from the comprehensive school; the father of one of the children from the comprehensive school, though he didn't know it; a butcher; Major Nye and Una Persson; another Man; a Displaced Person; "Flash" Gordon Gavin; a small painter; and several hundred other individuals not immediately identifiable, including a Colonel Pyat.

Jerry, suffering from a little paramnesia—a recurrent but brief condition to which, like Miss Brunner, he was subject—had the impression that he had met everyone before but couldn't place most of them. He also had the impression of having said everything before, but he recognised what was happening and paid no attention.

("So you've been in Lapland,") a fat bishop said. "So you've been in Lapland."

("Yes.") "Yes."

("What for?") "What for?"

("You won't believe me.") "You won't believe me."

("Tell me a convincing lie.") "Tell me a convincing lie."

("To study the similarities between the Ragnarok theme and the second law of thermodynamics.") "To study the similarities between the Ragnarok theme and the second law of thermodynamics." Jerry's mind jerked back onto its normal wavelength. "You know: the gods and men against the giants; fire against ice—heat against cold. *Ragnarok and the Heat Death of the Universe*, my next paper."

The fat bishop giggled, patted Jerry's bottom, and moved off to tell the embroidered anecdote to his colleagues.

The Swedish girl saw him. "Jerry! Where did you go?"

Jerry was in a gallant mood. "Sweden—I thought that was where you had gone."

"Ha, ha!"

"You're getting too close."

"What do you mean?"

Jerry gulped. "It's time that phrase was melted down for scrap."

"Jerry, this is Laurence." She brought the juicy youngster forward. He gave Jerry a juicy smile.

"Hello, Laurence." Jerry squeezed the youngster's hand, which immediately began to sweat. "Hmmm, fast reactions."

"Laurence has been streamlined," the Swedish girl said mockingly from behind the youngster. "No frontal lobes."

"That's the stuff to give 'em. Shall we dance?"

"If you don't think we'll look too conspicuous."

"Heavens to Betsy, what should it matter to us!"

They danced the chaver, a rather formal measure with minuet and frug influences. Jerry thought of Mr

Powys's last moments and felt he could sense the tiny figures of Marek and Miss Brunner having it away in the caverns of his mind. He got out as fast as he could, back to the wide world.

"You dance very gracefully," she smiled.

"Yes," he said. "What's your name?"

"Ulla."

"You're not chewing gum tonight."

"Not tonight."

He began to feel randy. He rolled his eyes. She laughed.

"It's a big party," she said. "Why so big?"

"Safety in numbers."

"Is it all for me?"

"As much as you can take."

"Aha!"

He began to feel blissful. He closed his eyes. Up and down went his long legs, round went his body, in and out went his hands, and they danced together. He chewed at her flavoured hair and stroked her thighs. They danced apart, pirouetting. He took her hand and twirled her again. Then he led her from the room. They climbed over the people on the stairs, pushed through the throngs on the landing, found the next flight less densely crowded all the way to the top, where there were only a few people holding glasses and talking. In his bedroom there was just enough space for the door to open. The rest of it was taken up by the *bed*.

He closed the door and threw many bolts. The room

was in complete darkness. They fell to biting each other.

"Oho!" she cried as his hand swam up her leg.

"Ha, ha!" he whispered, and he began softly to punch her warm body. They rolled about laughing and groaning. She was a bit of all right. He kissed her cheek. She tickled him on the chest. Then they lay back, exhausted and content.

It was nice in the darkness with the girl beside him. He rolled her a cigarette and lit it for her. He rolled one for himself. He had a flash of memory. "Una?"

When they had finished, he pinched the cigarettes out and put his arm around her, cradling her head. They fell asleep.

But he dreamed of Catherine, of Catherine. He dreamed of Catherine. Cath-er-ine. He merged into her and he *was* Catherine. Catherine with a dart in her heart. Catherine himself, and when Frank came along, red as a lobster, he arched her body for Frank. When Frank had joined them they walked in a summer garden, the three of them peaceful in her body. And Mum…

"How many can one body take?" He woke up before the dream became too crowded. He began to make love to Ulla. Or was it Una?

When they arose the following afternoon, they found the party beginning to warm up. They washed in the bathroom adjoining the bedroom, and Jerry left her to unlock his dressing room and put on fresh clothes.

They breakfasted on pâté and rye bread which the caterers had just brought in. Then they parted. Jerry picked up a discarded horror-film magazine and took it into the ground-floor room, where he sat on a cushion and read it. Next to him lay a cold Man with closed eyes. Someone had stepped on The Man's dropper. Someone else had removed his tights. He looked pretty funny.

When he had finished the magazine, Jerry wandered through the house and found the corpses of two Special Branch men. This intrusion annoyed him, and he kicked at the bodies for a moment. One of them had been garrotted, and the other didn't have a mark on him. Hans Smith, rather drunk, holding a bottle of wine, pointed at the unmarked Special Branch man. "Shock, old boy, shock. The rate it's taking them off they ought to set up a British Shock Research Institute, eh?"

"How long have you got, then?" asked Jerry.

"The doctors say a year, but I think less."

"It's best to."

"I don't think much of your friends, seriously, old boy. I had to ask one or two of them to leave—on your behalf, since I couldn't find you."

"Thank you, Mr Smith."

"Thank you, old boy."

In a corner the self-pitying albino was talking to Charlie Parker. "I was thinking of changing my name myself," he was saying. "How would you like to be called Pierro?"

Two of the warlocks had assembled the best part of the

comprehensive school teachers, pupils and parents. They wanted a virgin for a symbolic sacrifice. "Only *symbolic*, you understand."

The fourteen antique dealers from Portobello Road were enjoying the Polish french-polisher in a gang bang.

The Turkish and Persian lesbians sat straight-backed on cushions and looked on.

The Deep Fix were backing Little Miss Dazzle, and her small, true voice sang "Just What It Is", the melody weaving round and above the general noise of the party, counterpointing the screams and giggles and grunts and low moans. Jerry paused and listened to her.

She saw him and finished the song.

"This is your house?"

"Yes. That was nice."

"You're Mr Cornelius?"

"I am."

"Mr Cornelius, I believe you know Mr Crookshank, my agent. I haven't been able to get in touch with him for *weeks*."

Jerry felt sorry for Little Miss Dazzle, she looked so upset.

"I haven't seen him for some time either."

"Oh, dear. I've had offers from other agents, and I'll need to get someone soon or my career will be finished. But I—well, I got on so well with him. Where on earth is he?"

"The last I saw of him was in France—Normandy— the coast."

"He's abroad!"

"You could've fooled me." And, of course, she had. "I'm going out for a ride. Want to come?"

"Well—I came with three men. I met them on Fleet Street."

"I'm sure they won't mind if you're away for a few hours."

She gave him a sweet smile. "Oh, all right." She hooked her arm in his and they went out of the back of the house down to the garage. Jerry decided to use the Duesenberg.

In Battersea, as he drove towards the park, Jerry discovered the truth about Little Miss Dazzle. "Oh, well…" he said and put a comforting arm round her shoulders. She cuddled up.

The months of the party went by and Jerry circulated. The Suffolk fire-eater, who had experience in show business, took Little Miss Dazzle off his hands and became her agent, just in time.

Guests died or left and new ones came. Spring arrived, green and lovely, and the guests oozed into the garden. The catering firm first of all refused to accept a cheque for their monthly account; then they refused paper money, and Jerry had to pay them in sovereigns. He paid them with a secret grin.

The party continued to be catered for. The trucks, Jerry noted, drove through clearer streets, and there didn't seem to be as many people about as usual.

Jerry went back in one day and checked his calendar.

He was puzzled. It wasn't right. Not yet.

He took the calendar down and tore it across with a frown.

The morose Colonel Pyat was looking at him.

"What's the trouble?" He spoke moodily.

"Time," said Jerry. "Something wrong with the time."

"I don't follow you."

"It's moving too fast."

"I see."

"Don't bother," said Jerry, walking back into the main room, picking his way over the guests.

"I'd like to listen to what you're getting at." A psychiatrist followed him. "Honestly I would."

"Maybe you can tell me why so many people seem to have left London so soon."

"So soon—were you expecting them to leave?"

"I expected something like it."

"When?"

"I expected the first signs in a year or so."

"The first signs of what?"

"The breakup. It was bound to come, but…"

"Not so soon. An interesting idea. I thought we were bound to get straight again. Surely the economic crisis was only temporary. Europe's resources, manpower, *brain* power…"

"I was more optimistic." Jerry turned and grinned at the psychiatrist from Regent's Park.

"I see you have recovered your self-possession."

Jerry waved his hand round the room. "I wouldn't say that. You see most of what I possess."

The psychiatrist frowned.

"Well, what's your explanation?" Jerry asked him.

"I thought it was a temporary solution, as I said. This land rush I've heard about…"

"What's that?"

"Apparently there's been some sort of back-to-the-land movement, you know. From what I hear, the Scottish Highlands are like Blackpool beach in August, with everybody staking a claim. People seem to have lost faith in the pound and the government, such as it is."

"Very sensible. So the stockbrokers are stockbreeding and raising wheat."

"That seems to be about the size of it. Not that you can raise much wheat in the Highlands. But the same is true all over rural Britain—more people in the country than in the towns these days."

"Aha. This shouldn't have happened yet."

"Have I been missing out? Did anyone else anticipate this?"

Jerry shrugged.

"Maybe you've heard of this atom-bomb rumour?" the psychiatrist plugged on.

"Atom-bomb rumour? No, nothing." Jerry felt surprised. "Atom bombs?"

"One of the sheets reported a rumour that a maniac was threatening to bomb the European capitals."

"Go on!" Jerry jeered.

"I know—but these days you just don't know what to believe."

"I *thought* I did," said Jerry.

Soon London began to stink. There were power failures and failures of many other kinds. Jerry wasn't sufficiently concerned to check, but it seemed that the seat of government had been moved to Edinburgh. London, it appeared, had been abandoned. Jerry was prepared for this, and soon his private generators were going—years too soon, in his opinion. When the water was on, he pumped as much as he could into specially prepared rooftop reservoirs. Chemical toilets replaced the others. His guests increased for a few weeks, and then a hard core took up residence. Few left. There were few new arrivals.

What had happened to the country? The coalition government seemed ineffectual, unable to deal with anything at all. For a while it was a talking point, and then the party settled down again until July.

In July, Miss Brunner and Marek turned up at the party. Marek looked much younger and more ingenuous than Jerry remembered. At first he put it down to the Lapland winter and the poor light. But then he realised that Miss Brunner had found Dimitri's replacement.

"Congratulations," he said, leading his friends through the hall. It was full of marvellous perfume. "Where have you been all this time? By the look of things, Miss Brunner, you made good use of my father's secret."

She laughed. "Full use. The *gold* I've been converting recently. Chaos reigns, Mr Cornelius!"

"Or entropy, is it?" Marek smiled secretly.

"The process is getting going sooner than I thought…" Jerry led them to the second-floor bar and got them drinks.

"It is indeed, Mr Cornelius." She raised her glass. "And the toast is to Hermaphrodite!"

"Spare one for my father. He was some help to you."

"To Herr Cornelius the Elder and Hermaphrodite!" She called the toast in perfect Swedish.

10

"And what, for the record, was my father's powerful secret?"

"Something he learned in the war," she told him. "As you know, he was a talented man, part of the British scientific team that followed the Allies into Germany. They were very keen to discover just how far certain German scientific projects had got. They were relieved to find they hadn't got as far as they thought. But your father, with his eye on the main chance, discovered something that none of the others discovered."

"The underground cave system?" Jerry didn't know much about the war.

"No—this was much closer to home, although the caves were part of it. The Germans were working on an atomic reactor. At one stage, according to the records, they had been forced to decide whether to aim for an atomic engine or an atomic bomb. They decided on the engine— their resources, particularly the supply of uranium, were much more limited than ours, don't forget. The reactor was originally located in Berlin, but moved away when things began to get hot. It was captured by the Allies. That is the official story."

"The unofficial one?"

"There were two reactors, two projects—one for an engine and one for a bomb. They had produced bombs by the end of the war. They had decided on the Lapland caves—discovered by their 1937 expedition—as an ideal site for covering Russia and America. Those 'gun emplacements' you didn't bother to look at were launching pads for twenty A10 rockets fitted with atomic warheads. The microfilm was detailed and proved it. Copies were sent round Europe with a letter. They were authenticated. I was able to blackmail virtually every country in Europe without any of the others knowing."

"Why not Russia and America?"

"I wasn't interested in them, and they weren't psychologically prepared for it the way Europe was. Anyway, Russia captured the other reactor and must have known that there was a launching site somewhere—they might have guessed."

"Why weren't the missiles launched?"

"Hitler killed himself and the general in charge got cold feet, pulled out."

"So you got your hands on a lot of gold."

"Yes. It's back in circulation now, of course, but it did its job—and the confusion has precipitated the process."

"With you owning a lot of power."

"And a lot of people. I'm over here recruiting scientists, bringing work to hundreds—thousands, what with the industries concerned."

"You're building the computer?"

"In the Lapland caves."

"What about the bombs?"

Miss Brunner laughed. "Apart from the fact that the rocket machinery was corroded, accelerated by the vapour from the hot lake, the uranium in the warheads had been hastily refined—you know the trouble they were having with their heavy-water systems."

"They wouldn't go off."

"They didn't have a chance to test them, you see."

Jerry laughed and laughed.

"I see you've got a lot of scientists and technicians here," she said. "Do you mind if I do a bit of quiet recruiting while I'm at it?"

"Help yourself. The party's all yours. I've finished with it now."

ABIOLOGISTS (3), ACAROLOGIST (1), ACOLOGISTS (2), ACROLOGIST (1), ADENOLOGISTS (5), AESTHOPHYSIOLOGISTS (6), AETIOLOGISTS (2), ALETHIOLOGIST (1), ALCHEMIST (1), AMPHIBIOLOGISTS (10), ANATRIPSOLOGIST (1), ANDROLOGISTS (10), ANGIOLOGISTS (4), ANORGANOLOGISTS (3), ANTHROPOLOGISTS (4), ANTHROMORPHOLOGIST (1), ARCHAEOLOGISTS (4), ARCHOLOGISTS (6), AREOLOGISTS (2), ARTHROLOGISTS (4), ASTHENOLOGISTS (2), ASTROLITHOLOGIST (1), ASTROLOGERS (7), ASTROMETEOROLOGIST (1), ATMOLOGISTS (2), AUDIOLOGIST (1), AUXOLOGISTS (6).

"Your want list." Jerry studied the pages. There were twenty-six categories, corresponding to the letters of the alphabet.

"I've filled most of it," she said. "I heard of your party through a histologist I hired—one of his colleagues was at it."

"So you came along to try to complete the list. Some ark you're building!"

She looked ecstatic. "I'm the ark—I'm the deluge! Within the year! I've had the hot lake roofed over, laboratories and plants put up. DUEL is the most marvellous thing you've ever seen! Decimal Unit Electronic Linkage. It will fill half the cave system. At this moment it has the capabilities of any machine in existence, except that it's much faster. We'll complete the assembly in another year. And that's when the real work will begin!"

"What's so different about it?"

Marek grinned at Miss Brunner. "It incorporates a number of unprecedented features," he said. "To begin with, each of its units, instead of being a simple on/off switch, is capable of ten magnetic states, so that the computer operates on a decimal instead of a binary basis. This is what gives it its already tremendously increased power. In addition to this, it utilises ingenious linkages which apparently," he chuckled, "not even the designer of the human brain thought of! This can open up an entirely new investigation of the material world. Hints of all kinds of unexpected relationships are appearing from the computer's calculations. Ultimately DUEL will probe beyond the root of matter itself. Miss Brunner has forged—"

"A scientific tool—not a glorified abacus!" Miss Brunner folded her want list. "DUEL is much more than a computer, Mr Cornelius."

"Yes indeed, Miss Brunner," said Marek.

"I couldn't contribute." Jerry winked at her.

"Couldn't you?"

"You're at it again!"

"Would you have it any other way?"

"All other ways. You want more than information from DUEL, Miss Brunner."

"I don't want information from DUEL—not ultimately. It is DUEL who wants information. I want—a result. Conclusive data, and more."

"You are ambitious."

Marek's eyes shone. "But what an ambition, Herr Cornelius!"

Jerry looked sideways at her little familiar.

"You want to come to see DUEL?" Miss Brunner seemed unusually eager.

"You seem unusually eager," said Jerry.

"Aha!" Marek's eyes watered.

"I think I'd like to leave London for a bit."

"The smell," she said. "I suppose we are indirectly responsible for that."

Jerry grinned at her somewhat admiringly. "Well, yes, I suppose you are."

"This was a gift-wrapped, throwaway age, Mr Cornelius. Now the gift wrapping is off, it's being thrown away."

"It's certainly perishable." Jerry wrinkled his nose.

"Oh, *you*!"

"I won't join you just yet," Jerry decided. "I haven't been into the centre of town for a while. I'll see what things are like there. If they're better, I'll stay for as long as I can."

• • • • •

After Jerry had left, Miss Brunner and Marek ranged the party, mixing in but always staying close together.

After a bit they found Jerry's bedroom and went in.

"He does himself well," said Miss Brunner, sitting on the bed and bouncing up and down.

"Why did you let him go?"

"He hasn't been downtown lately. It will do him good."

"But you might lose him."

"No. There are a limited number of places he will go to. I know them all."

She reached out and pulled Marek towards the bed. He crawled up it towards the pillows and then lay on his back, staring at the ceiling. His face was blank as Miss Brunner flung herself on top of him with a throaty cry.

"Time for a last coming together, my tender," she whispered as she nibbled his ear.

Marek let out a great sigh, expelling all the air from his lungs.

A short while later, looking better than she had, Miss Brunner supervised the men she had hired. They were rapidly crating up Jerry's threads and taking them down to a waiting van.

While she supervised, 'Flash' Gordon Gavin passed by wearing Marek's clothes. She gave him a swift glance. He noticed and turned, smiling rather wistfully. "I found them in the bedroom. Nobody seemed to own them, so..."

He fingered the cloth. "Are they suitable?"

"Oh, I should think so," she said.

Jerry felt uneasy driving the Duesenberg through the ill-frequented streets. London was littered, London was grey, though here and there a crowd, extravagantly dressed, would give beauty to the picture. To Jerry, as he passed them, each crowd seemed a single unit, a composite creature, many-limbed and many-headed. Nearer the centre of town the crowds were bigger creatures, getting bigger as he came close to Piccadilly Circus. Jerry felt alone, and the crowd-creatures seemed menacing.

In the Chicken Fry he found that chicken was off. It was flavoured algae and like it. He didn't bother. The big place was poorly lit, and he sat near the back in shadow. He was the only customer—the only person, except for the Maltese counter-hand, who never looked up.

As the light grew fainter, a crowd came in, its thick, snakelike body squeezing through the glass double doors and flowing out to fill the interior. It frightened Jerry, and Jerry loved crowds. But he was not in this one and did not want to be. It flowed forward and detached part of itself at him. He got up quickly, drawing his needle gun. At that moment, he wanted a gun with plenty of dum-dum bullets. The Part grinned slyly, and the rest of it mirrored the grin, all its heads turned towards him.

Jerry drew a number of shallow breaths, and tears filled his eyes as he stood there looking into the face of the crowd.

The Part sat down where Jerry had been sitting, and Jerry recognised it then.

"Shades?" he whispered.

"Who?" whispered back The Part.

"Shades!"

"No."

"Who are you?"

"What?"

"You!"

"No."

Jerry shot The Part in the white throat. Spots of blood made a necklace round the pale flesh. The crowd gasped and began to undulate. Jerry pushed through it. It broke and re-formed behind him until he was in the centre. Then, when he tried to push on, it gave like the walls of a stomach but it didn't break. It began to press inward.

He shot some more needles into it and hacked and clawed his way towards the door. Outside was the big, safe Duesenberg. He wept as he made the street, turned and saw a hundred white faces, all with identical expressions, pressed against the glass staring at him.

Trembling, sick, he climbed into the car and started it up. The crowd did not follow him, but its heads turned to watch him until he was out of sight.

Jerry had pulled himself together by the time he had reached Trafalgar Square. He was not going to give up until he had tried the Friendly Bum.

He heard the music at the entrance where the dead neon sign drooped. It was slowed-down music, dragging, monotonous, introspective. Tentatively he descended the stairs. The spotlights had been turned onto the stage and there sat the heavy-eyed musicians, moulded onto or around their instruments. The pianotron played deep, sonorous, over-sustained chords. In the centre of the place stood a tired pyramid of flesh that moved to the slow rhythm, near quiescent, and the temperature of the place seemed sub-zero.

It hadn't lasted, Jerry thought. It should not have reached this stage until he was at least forty. He was a fool to have helped Miss Brunner to accelerate the process. It left him adrift.

Had Miss Brunner known this would happen to him? How long had she included him in her plans? How much was he a factor in her programme? He had been on top, right on top, at the beginning, when they had first met. She had become wiser, then? Or he had underestimated her.

"You have lost the advantage, Mr Cornelius," she said from behind him. He turned and looked at her standing at the top of the stairs, her legs as widely spaced as the tight skirt would allow, her long red hair drawn back behind the ears of her pointed face, her small, sharp teeth exposed. "You have a choice," she said, and she spread her hand towards the pyramid.

"Where is Marek?"

"Where Dimitri is. And Jenny."

"He didn't die at the house?"

"He will never die."

"You won't take me in like the others." He smiled nervously.

"A good try, but you can do even better. I won't—not like the others. I promise."

He knew he was about to vomit. He tried to stop himself then he turned and his body shook mightily as he spewed. He felt her touch him and was too weak to shake her off. His head ached with the intensity of a migraine attack. "Get it out of your system," he heard her say distantly as she led him up the stairs. "Will you bring the car round please, bishop?"

12

He drove according to her quiet instructions and obeyed her when she sat him in the cabin of her plane, a handy Hawker-Siddeley executive jet.

"You will soon be almost your old self," she promised as they flew towards the North Pole.

They landed on the lush, swampy plain dominated by a huge sun, a swelling circle of blood on the horizon. It was hot, and mosquitoes swirled in thick clouds round them. She led him along a wooden catwalk through the marsh. She comforted him and calmed him as they moved towards the mountains. She fed strength to him through her hand, which tightly clasped his. He was duly grateful.

"I've had your entire wardrobe shipped here," she told him. "All your identities."

"Thank you, Miss Brunner."

By the time they reached the cave he had dropped her hand, and he followed her with a jauntier step into the forcefully lighted cavern. It was large and high, though not so large and high as he had thought when he had first traversed it in darkness.

Farther down, buildings were being erected and gangs of men moved busily. The cavern moaned with all the voices of all the power tools, large and small.

"You own a lot of talent." It was the first comment Jerry had made since their meeting at the Friendly Bum.

"You're feeling better. Good. Do I seem less of a threat now?" They walked on.

The hot-lake cavern had a sheet of steel-hard plastic material as its floor. Great slabs of neon ranged its walls, and fat pipes curled among the neon lamps like the World Snake at rest. The roof was still hard to make out, the more so since it was obscured by cables, pipes and gridworks. Dwarfed by the cavern, hundreds of people darted, antlike, about.

"It's rather like an old Fritz Lang film, isn't it?" She paused to look around her. He didn't understand the reference. "Or the one they did of *Things to Come.*" Another reference that escaped him. She looked into his face. "I saw them as a child," she said.

It was the first defensive comment she had made since their meeting at the Friendly Bum.

"Yes, I'm beginning to feel better," said Jerry, and he grinned at her suddenly.

"There's no need to be rude," she said. "Give a man an inch…"

Jerry loosened his muscles and drew a deep breath.

"You almost had me that time."

"What makes you think I wanted you?"

"You want something from me."

"You should be flattered. I have most of the best brains in Europe working for me—and as many from other continents as I could hire or make enthusiastic."

"A noble enterprise. Directed where?"

"Would you be surprised to learn I had a son, Mr Cornelius?"

"Encore!"

"How do you feel?"

Jerry didn't know. He felt odd, but he wasn't going to say so. "But you look so *young*."

"I keep myself young, one way and another."

"You could follow it up, Miss Brunner, if you're as well informed about me as you appear to be."

"Your father got around."

"So did my mum. She's Russian, you know."

"What do you want me to say, Mr Cornelius? The man I'm referring to did have a connection with your father—Leslie Baxter."

"The so-called psychobiologist my father took under his wing. He's a nut."

"They stopped a great many subsidies. He'd been living off them."

"Leslie Baxter's your son? He picked my father's brains."

"Do you mean he learned everything your father could teach him and then went off to do better on his own?"

"Have it your way. Why did you tell me?"

"That's a very direct question for you. Did I say something to upset you?"

"Fuck you!"

"In time, Mr Cornelius, we'll see about that. Look." She pointed. "We've torn down all those Nazi buildings—jerry-built stuff."

"You should have preserved them for posterity."

"I have a different kind of posterity in mind."

"Why?"

"I've forgotten the question."

"Why did you tell me Baxter was your son?"

"Are you mellowing, Mr Cornelius? Be a trifle more patient and I'll explain."

"What happened to Dimitri and Jenny and Marek?"

"They weren't the only ones."

"They were the only ones I knew."

"They became absorbed in something—and forgot me."

"Oh, shit…"

She laughed. "Come and look at DUEL—the pride of Laplab."

DUEL was huge. Its great, angular, nearly featureless bulk stretched upward for nearly 200 feet. It was growing round the three walls of the far cavern in a green semicircle covering at least a third of a mile. At its base, teams of technicians sat, like a pool of office girls, tapping out data and feeding it in.

"Nothing coming out, I see," said Jerry, leaning back to look up at it.

"Oh, not for a while yet," she said. "There's another cavern, you know—one you didn't find on our first trip."

The entrance was small, barely higher than Jerry. A steel airlock had been fitted into it. "To keep a constant pressure inside," she said, "and shut out smells and noise."

They went through. On the other side of the airlock was a cave about 200 feet high and 500 feet in diameter. It was lighted with yellow simulated sunshine, and part of it had been cultivated into a flower garden. The air was fresh and pleasant. In the centre stood a white, terraced building that looked familiar. It was extravagant, baroque, with a twin-towered Byzantine-Gothic appearance. There were crosses on top of the towers.

"A touch of vulgarity in my personality," she said as he stared at it smiling. "Do you recognise it?"

"I think so."

"It's Hearst's palace of San Simeon. I had it transported from the States stone by stone. He was almost as big a collector as I am, though with different tastes on the whole. These things come and go, you know. Want to see the inside?"

They walked up the steps and through the huge doors. They walked through the high, bare rooms. There was no furniture at all on the ground floor.

"I thought you were doing a Chinese-box trick—you should have had a smaller house inside this one."

"That's an idea. I might do it—we could probably

get two more in and there I'd be, cosy in a three-roomed bijou, right at the centre."

"Is that how many layers you need?"

"I don't need any *layers*, Mr Cornelius. Your brother Frank was of that bent. Do you know I found some more of his papers? He believed that the human race originated inside the globe. How's that for a big womb fixation? He didn't come here just to check what he found on the microfilm, you know."

"You don't like caves yourself, though. You didn't want to go on, as I remember."

"You're right. This isn't a womb for me, Mr Cornelius—it is a womb for DUEL and what it will create."

"What will it create?"

"The ultimate joke."

"Fine words." He followed behind her as she walked up the great sweeping staircase.

"Do you know what you'll find soon behind the blank wall of that computer?"

He paused and turned leaning on the banister. "Not a giant abacus—you told me at the party."

"Living human brains that can function for hundreds of years if I need them that long. That's the sort of sophistication going into DUEL!"

"Ah, that's corny. Is that your ultimate joke?"

"No, it's just part of the food routine."

"You're getting earnest, Miss Brunner."

"You're right. Come on."

In a smallish room on the third floor she showed him

his wardrobe. He inspected it. "All here," he said. "You work fast."

"I arranged it as soon as you left your house."

"If you don't mind, since you've been so thoughtful, I'll have a bath and change."

"Go ahead. We've got hot water and central heating laid on by nature."

"I bet that's all."

"More or less."

She showed him to a bathroom and stood watching him wash himself. He wasn't embarrassed by her clinical once-over, but it didn't help him to relax.

She followed him back to the room where his wardrobe was and helped him on with his jacket. He felt better.

"What you need is a good home-cooked meal," she said.

"Play it your way."

The food was delicious and the wine perfect. He had never enjoyed a meal so much. "The calf is fatted," he said as he sat back.

"You're becoming naïve."

"Now you're trying to worry me again."

"You had a big supply of food and drink at your place in Holland Park."

"I won't use it now. The breakdown was too fast."

"But the buildup will come sooner, Mr Cornelius."

"That hasn't got anything to do with me—you forced the pace. I was a creature of my time; now I've no natural environment. That's what you've done to me."

She looked at her watch. "Let's go and meet someone you know."

They left San Simeon and returned through the airlock, passing DUEL and going out onto the surface covering the hot lake, towards one of the new buildings.

"The quarters are not austere," she said. "I think we'll find this mutual friend at home."

Inside one of the blocks they climbed stairs, Miss Brunner apologising that the elevators weren't working yet. On the second floor she led him down a corridor and knocked on one of the simulated-wood Formica doors.

After a short wait, it was opened by a man dressed only in a turban and a towel round his waist. He looked like a fakir. It was Professor Hira. "*Hello*, Mr Cornelius!" He beamed. "I had heard you were in these parts, old man. Good afternoon, Miss Brunner. An honour! Come in!"

The bed-sitting room was bright with Swedish furniture—bed, desk, chairs, bookcase, a couple of scatter rugs. The Hindu sat down on the bed and they took the chairs.

"What are you up to, Mr Cornelius?" He slipped the towel off and sat back comfortably on the bed. Jerry looked at him and smiled to himself. Hira was a kind of link unit between himself and Miss Brunner. Was it significant?

"I'm just an observer," Jerry said. "Or you could even say I've come seeking sanctuary."

"Ha, ha! What a magnificent example! I cannot tell you how delighted I was to be offered a position here by Miss Brunner. That you should think of me, Miss Brunner, still baffles me."

"I haven't forgotten Delhi, professor," she said. "You have special talents."

"Good of you to say so. Perhaps I will be able to make better use of them shortly. There hasn't been much for me to do so far—a few interesting equations, a little speculation; I am not yet in my stride."

"Don't worry, you soon will be."

He snorted, amused. "My God, I never thought I would have to brush up on my Sanskrit for professional reasons. That old man in the next flat—Professor Martin— he is a better scholar than I!" He pointed a finger at Jerry. "Remember what we talked about in Angkor last year?"

"Very well, now you mention it. We must both have precognition, professor. I find it a little disturbing here and there."

"Yes—I know what you mean. But we have faith in Miss Brunner, eh?" He leaned back, smiling and shaking his head at her. She smiled at him, a little faintly.

"Oh, I'm just administration." Her smile broadened.

"You said it!" Jerry introduced a wrong note.

"It's time we were leaving." She got up. "I hope the three of us will be able to get together later, professor."

"Oh, I certainly hope so too, Miss Brunner." He saw them out. "*Au revoir*!"

"*Au revoir*, professor," said Miss Brunner.

"And now where?" Jerry asked.

"Back to San Simeon. You must be tired."

"I'd like to know if I can leave when I want to."

"I'm hoping your curiosity will make you stay for a bit—and you've nowhere else to go, have you?" They went down the stairs.

"No. You've really got me where you want me, I suppose."

"That's where you're wrong."

As they left the block and began to walk back towards DUEL he sighed. "I thought I'd remain comparatively static while my surroundings were in a state of flux. But I appear to have been caught in the flux. It's just no good making preparations. On the other hand, I don't like being aimless while the world is aimless, and my old aim is gone."

"What was that?"

"To survive."

"I might be able to supply an aim or two if you're keen."

"I'll listen, Miss Brunner, at any rate." As she operated the airlock control, he suppressed an urge to reach out for her. "Things are becoming peculiar," he said as he followed her into the opening. "What will I think of next!"

"You're talking to yourself, you know," she pointed out. They emerged on the other side, and the smell of the flowers was exquisite.

"Haven't I always? But whose internal monologue is this? Yours or mine?"

"You're getting warmer. We're a finely balanced pair,

Mr Cornelius. Have you thought about it? Neither of us keeps the upper hand for long. I'm not used to it."

"I know what you mean. I'm afraid."

Jerry became thoughtful, as best he could. He was beginning to feel pretty.

"This is our bedroom." She stood in the doorway behind him. There were shutters on the windows and they were closed. The bed was a four-poster with curtains drawn. She shut the door.

"I'm not sure," he said. He wasn't scared and he wasn't particularly randy—he just wasn't sure, in a cool kind of way.

She moved towards him and pressed herself against his back, stroking his stomach with her long, pale hands. He stood there passively for a moment, then said, "Did you know you haven't any sex appeal at all? I've wondered how you made out—with Dimitri and Marek and the others."

"No sex appeal," she murmured. "That's the whole secret."

"And here I am." He glimmed the room. "What does it make me? A sucker, a patsy, a fall guy…"

"You underestimate yourself, Mr Cornelius." She walked over to the bed and pulled a cord. The curtains parted and there, spread out on the eiderdown, was the loveliest white bridal gown he had ever seen.

"Who's it for? You or me?"

"That choice, Mr Cornelius, is entirely up to you."

He shrugged and took his jacket off as she unzipped her skirt and stepped out of it.

"Let's toss for it, Miss Brunner."

"That suits me, Mr Cornelius."

He found a coin in his pocket, flipped it. She called: "Incubus!"

"Succubus," he said. "Lucky old me."

Two weeks later and hand in hand they walked among silver birches beneath the hot blue sky beneath the big red sun. The shining lake stretched away out of sight, and the land was green and brown, at perfect peace. The only visible life, apart from themselves and the mosquitoes, was a large partridge circling high, guarding her nest.

Miss Brunner waved a hand behind her to indicate the ancient mountains that hid her mighty projects.

The mountains were streaked with glaciers, topped with snow, time-begrimed and worn.

"We had some trouble on Number 14 Section's subsidiary circuits. That's Professor Hira's section. I had to do some fast calculating—the correlation monitors started improvising. Too much feedback potential there, I think."

"No kidding. You expected some setbacks—I mean, it's a big project, DUEL..."

"The biggest, Mr Cornelius." She squeezed his hand. "The," she sighed, "total sum, the quintessence of all human knowledge, the definitive data. Yum, yum. And that'll be just the start."

They wandered, this shepherd and his lass—though neither was quite sure who was who—beside the lake. Fish were jumping and the gorse was high. The world was warm and restful and an infinity of mountains, forests and lakes where night could not fall and it was always day, hazy and lazy.

The mosquitoes enjoyed it too as they sat on the arms and faces of their hosts, inserting their probosces through the skin and into the veins, drinking the thick, rich blood to satiation, raising little hard hillocks on the flesh as monuments to their visitation. The living was easy and the flesh pounded warmly on the bone, the veins and arteries functioned smoothly, nerves and synapses did their stuff, organs performed their proper duties, and nobody would have guessed, least of all the mosquitoes, that skeletons lurked under cover.

"The start of what, though?"

"You're still not with me?"

"Oh, I am, I am."

"The funniest thing," she replied. "Think about it. Think what's beyond this green and pleasant land, these uninhabited pastures. The world crumbles to cold sand and the sixty-minute hour is a thing of the past, the twenty-four-hour day has been devalued. There has to be a bridge, Mr Cornelius, between now and the past-future. That's what I intend to build—the bridge."

"Blow me down. And what's my part again?"

"I didn't say. Don't worry, Mr Cornelius, you're fixed up destiny-wise. Drift, drift…"

"If I don't?"

She turned and looked into his face. "Will you do something—a favour?"

"Things are moving again. What?"

"My son dreams of glory. He had only a small part of my resources and information, yet it is that small part I need, by God. He refuses to give it up—the last piece in the jigsaw. Would you go to England, to the Wamering Research Institute, and secure me that piece?"

"It's a long trip. Why should he hand it over to me?"

"Oh, he won't. You would probably, in the long run, have to kill him to get it."

"I wouldn't mind killing him?"

"No."

"Oh-ho, Miss *Brunner*."

"Don't wag fingers at *me*, Mr Cornelius!"

"I'll kill him, then. What do you want there?"

"Nothing much—nothing heavy. A few notes. He published prodigiously, but he kept those notes back. They're the fill-in data I need."

"I'm far too tired to go by myself. I want a chauffeur all the way. I'll need to conserve my energy."

"You're getting lazy."

"Weary, weary, weary. I like it here." He stretched and stared out over the glinting lake.

"I've got you a good little gun," she wheedled. "The Smith and Wesson .41 Magnum Manstopper. It's a handy gun—not too heavy, not too light. Just the trick."

"Is it noisy?"

"Not very."

"Does it kick hard?"

"Not much."

"Well, I'll use it. But I'm nervous of gunpowder guns."

"You lost your other one."

"I know I did."

"Let's go back. I'll show it to you and you can try it out. Blam! Blam!"

"Oh, Jesus, those gleaming eyes!"

"Har! Har!" She began to run towards the mountains. He paused for only a moment or so before he loped off after her.

Disappointed mosquitoes saw them disappear into the caves.

13

Jerry huddled in his coat as the pilot taxied the plane off the small private runway a couple of miles beyond Kiruna. The Iron Mountain, source of Kiruna's wealth—source, indeed, of Kiruna—was soon below them as they headed south.

In Kent they landed and a Dodge Dart and driver were waiting for them. The driver, as silent as the pilot, drove Jerry through a land of drifters, smoke and disturbance, a warped landscape that he only glimpsed as he hunched in his seat and let himself be carried towards the Wamering Research Institute. The place was on the South Coast, just outside a run-down seaside resort. Jerry had memories of the place—white-washed Regency and the sweet smell of spun sugar and frozen custard, cold promenade and green railings, pale lights at night and the silhouette of the pier, faint music, blue cafés and open-top buses. Even as a child he had disliked it all, had turned inland when left to himself.

The Wamering Research Institute stood on a slope of the Sussex Downs. On the top of the hill was an estate that seemed to have been built during the war. It still had a temporary look about it. The road took them through its concrete streets—a small grid of blocks with two-storeyed houses, white walls and dull red roofs. Puzzled eyes looked out of hollow faces at them. The people stood in family groups—a Father, a Mother, a Son and a Daughter—arms folded, heads turning a little as they passed. A stunned, wronged place.

"Have you got Mr Pipe the Plumber?" Jerry turned to the driver.

"Nearly there, sir." The driver kept his eyes on the road.

Depressed and in a killing mood, Jerry let the driver drop him off at the gates of the institute's grounds. The buildings—some of metal, some of plastic, some of concrete—could be seen painted grey and green in weatherproof paints. The concrete ones looked the oldest. The institute seemed to have been established before Leslie Baxter had taken over the buildings.

Jerry trod the tarmac towards the institute, gun in pocket. He reached the main building, rough concrete with a steel door fairly recently installed. He pressed the bell and heard a faint buzzing within. The battery was running low.

A girl answered the door, sliding a Judas window.

Her head looked up and down. "Yes?"

"I'm Jerry Cornelius."

"Come again?"

"Cornelius. Dr Baxter will recognise the name. I

would like to see him. I have something that my father should have given him before he died."

"Dr Baxter is very busy indeed. We are doing some important experiments, sir. It is vital work."

"Vital, eh?"

"Dr Baxter believes we can save Britain."

"With hallucimats?"

"I'll give him your name—but we have to be careful who we let in. Hang on a minute."

"Tell him that my plan will radically alter his research."

"You're serious—he will know you?"

Jerry tired of his joke. "Yes."

He waited for more than twenty minutes before the girl returned. "Dr Baxter will be pleased to see you," she said, opening the steel door.

Jerry padded into a square reception hall and followed the girl down a corridor like any other corridor. The girl looked strange to him, with long curly hair and a full skirt, seam-free stockings and high heels. It was a long time ago when he'd last seen such a sexy girl. She was a positive anachronism and made him feel slightly sick. He restrained himself from hauling out his gun.

A door was labelled DR BAXTER; the room contained Dr Baxter. Nice and neat.

Leslie Baxter was only slightly older than Jerry. Well dressed and kept, tall and pale, gaunt and haunted. His body was bigger than Jerry's, gave out a greater impression of power, but even Jerry noticed that they were quite similar in appearance.

"You are Dr Cornelius's son, I take it? I'm glad to meet you." His voice was tired, vibrant. "Which son?"

"Jeremiah, Dr Baxter."

"Oh, yes, Jeremiah. We never—"

"—met. No."

"You were always away—"

"—from home while you were there. Yes. So you never met Frank either?"

"Only your sister Catherine. How is she?"

"Dead."

"I'm so sorry—she was very young. Was it—?"

"—an accident? Of sorts. I killed her."

"You killed her? Not deliberately?"

"Who knows? Shall we discuss the matter I came about?"

Baxter sat down behind his desk. Jerry sat on the other side.

"You seem distraught, Mr Cornelius. Could I get you a drink, something like that?"

"No, thanks. Your receptionist said you were doing some very important work. Work—vital to the nation?"

Baxter looked proud. "Perhaps to the world. I give your father credit for all the original work, you know."

"But you're getting the positive results, eh?"

"That's about the size of it." Baxter flashed Jerry a puzzled look. "Our research into useful hallucinogens and hallucimats is reaching a conclusion. We shall soon be ready."

"Useful in what way?"

"They will reproduce mass-conditioning effects, Mr Cornelius. Mass-conditioning that will make people sane again—saner, in fact, than they have ever been before. Our machines and drugs can do this—or will be able to within a few months. We are, in fact, largely beyond the research stage and are producing several models that have proved absolutely workable. They will help to turn the world onto a sane track. We'll be able to restore order, salvage the nation's resources…"

"It's got a familiar ring. Don't you realise it's a waste of time?" Jerry's hand stroked the butt of his S&W .41. "It's over—Europe only points the course of the rest of the world. Entropy's setting in. Or so they say."

"Why should that be true?"

"It's Time—it's all used up."

"This is metaphysical nonsense!"

"Very likely."

"What's your real purpose here?"

"Your mother wants the missing data—the stuff you didn't publish."

"Mother—? What should she want with—? My *mother*?"

"Miss Brunner. Don't mess about, Dr Baxter." Jerry smoothed the gun from his pocket and flicked the safety catch.

"Miss who?"

"Brunner. You've got some secret stuff you haven't published, haven't you?"

"What's that to you?"

"Where is it?"

"Mr Cornelius, I don't intend to tell you. You are disturbed. I will fetch the receptionist."

"Hold it."

"Put the gun—"

"—away, Mr Cornelius. It's like doing the Junior Crossword. No. Miss Brunner wants that information. You have refused to let her have it. She has authorised me to collect it from you."

"Authorised? What's your authorisation?"

"You fell into that one." Jerry laughed. "This!" He waved the gun. "Where's that information?"

Baxter glanced towards a filing cabinet on his right.

"There?" Jerry queried a little petulantly. Was Baxter going to give in so easily? Baxter looked away hastily. Yes, it was probably there.

"No," said Baxter.

"I believe you. Then where is it?"

"It—was destroyed."

"Liar!"

"Mr Cornelius. This is farcical. I have really important work to do…"

"It's all farce, Dr Baxter." Jerry levelled the gun at Baxter's stomach as the man rose to reach for a phone. "Freeze. Don't move. Stay exactly where you are."

"This *is* a joke. What did you say?"

"Freeze. Don't move. Stay exactly where you are."

"It wasn't what you said—it must have been your tone of voice."

"My main assignment from your mother was to get those documents. My main intention is to kill you."

"Oh, no. We had those steel doors installed to protect—we were safe—I had to let you in! Mr Cornelius— I'm sure you have never met my mother."

"Miss Brunner?"

"The name is only vaguely familiar, I assure you."

"You're sweating," said Jerry.

"I'm not—well, wouldn't you be? I don't know a Miss Brunner!" He screamed as the gun banged and the slug splatted into his belly. "Mr Cornelius! It isn't true! My mother couldn't—I was born in Mitcham—my father was in the Home Guard!"

"A likely story." Jerry shot him again, *bang!*

"And my mother worked in the margarine factory. Mr and Mrs Baxter—Dahlia Gardens, Mitcham. You can look them up."

Bang!

"*It's true!*" Baxter seemed to realise that he was full of large bullet holes. His eyes glazed. He fell forward over the desk.

The girl was hammering on the door. "Dr Baxter! Dr Baxter! What is it?"

"Something's going wrong," Cornelius shouted back. "Just a minute."

He opened the door and let her in. "Were you the only one who heard the noise?" He closed the door as she gasped and stared at the body on the desk.

"Yes—everyone else is in the lab. What—?"

Jerry shot her in the back at the base of the spine. She was silent for a moment. Screamed. Blacked out or died at once, you could never be quite sure.

Jerry crossed to the filing cabinet, pocketing the gun. It took him half an hour of careful leafing to find the files he wanted. But Dr Baxter, for all his faults, had been a tidy chap.

Jerry went out of the room with the file under his arm, a natty figure in his black car coat and tight black trousers, down the passage, through the reception hall, out of the main door and down the drive. He felt considerably better, in spite of the unpleasant smell of cordite in his nostrils and the bruised feeling of his right hand. He hadn't liked the shooting part very much.

The Dodge Dart, electric-blue and powerful, was waiting. The driver had the engine running as Jerry climbed in.

"Any trouble, sir?"

"No. With luck they'll never have a suspicion of who we were. Hadn't we better go fast now?"

"No sense in going too fast on these roads, sir."

"But someone may come after us."

"That's not very likely, sir. There's a lot of violent death about, sir. I mean, take me. I'm an ex-policeman. You can't blame the police, sir. They're an overburdened body of men."

"I suppose they must be."

They went back to the airfield in silence. Whose mother was who?

14

"No, of course he wasn't my son." Miss Brunner leafed eagerly through the file. They were in her office at Casa Grande. Jerry sat on the table watching her.

"You're just saying that now." He swung his legs.

"Try not to be so bitchy, kitten." She grinned as she extracted a document and scanned it. "This is the real stuff. Good for you."

"You and your bloody gun!"

"It wasn't my finger on the trigger."

"Don't be so sure."

"Calm down. You're not the Jerry Cornelius I knew."

"You can say that again. You and your bloody gun!"

"Blam! Blam!" She put the papers down. "You're just tired, Mr Cornelius. I had to get you to go. You were the only person who would recognise the stuff I wanted."

"You should have been more straightforward about it!"

"I couldn't be. Could you?"

"It's not right."

"You're whining, feathers!"

"Sod me, you'd be wh—" He pulled himself together. "I'm not sure I'm happy, Miss Brunner."

"What's happiness, Mr Cornelius? You need a change."

"I don't need any more, Miss Brunner. That's for sure."

"A change of scenery, that's all. There's nothing more for you to do here for a while. I have everything ready. It's just donkey work for a few months. I might come along too, when I've tidied up."

"Where do you want me to go?"

"Nowhere. It's up to you."

"I'll think it over."

She walked up to him and cupped his face in her hands. "How can you? What have you got to think with? Your tapes are stale, your clothes are tired—there's only *me*!"

He took her hands away from his face. "Only you?"

"You're failing fast. Not enough people, not enough stimuli. What have you got to live on, you bloody little vampire!"

"Me a vampire! You—Dimitri, Marek, Jenny and how many others? Me too, maybe…"

"Some realist you are, Mr Cornelius. Look at you— all self-pity and emotion!"

"It's catching then?"

"Don't lay it at my door."

"You're pretty hip yourself." He dropped off the table, feeling limp. "By God, I don't like it!"

Her voice became soft, and she began to stroke his arm. "I know some of it's my fault. Calm down, calm down. Cry if it helps."

He did; it didn't. He was being suckered skilfully, and he knew enough to know it. He broke away weeping and ran for the door. As it closed softly, automatically, behind him, she picked up the empty Smith and Wesson with a sigh that was half disappointment, half satisfaction.

"He's giving me too much credit," she said aloud. "I only hope things stay on schedule or we've all had it."

Jerry drove a Snow Trac at its top speed of 15 mph over the uneven countryside towards the distant village where he might get a place on a tourist bus. He drove south, away from the sun.

To him, Europe beyond Sweden had become not Miss Brunner's cold sand but a boiling sea of chaos soon to spread through Finland and Denmark, if it had not done so already. Not only was he physically enervated, but his mind was out of gear and exploding on all systems. It was awash with dark colours and fragments of dreams and memories. Only a small portion still operated logically, and logic had never been his strong point. He was neither fleeing nor going anywhere; he was simply moving—perhaps questing for prey like the mosquitoes buzzing round the outside of the cab, perhaps not.

The dreams and memories conflicted, and occasionally he would feel ill and weaker than ever as the thought came that they might all be wrong—even Baxter; that there was a simpler reason for it all. Yet if it were madness they had, then they shared it with too many others, and Miss Brunner had the power to make her fantasy reality. It had happened before. He remembered the families he had seen on his way to Wamering, and this image was superimposed on that of the pulsating pyramid of flesh he had seen in the Friendly Bum.

He reached Kvikjokk and there were no buses— just a couple of students from the tourist hotel driving a borrowed Volvo back to Lund. He found some sterling in his pockets and offered it in return for a lift to Stockholm. They laughed at the money.

"It's worthless. But we'll give you a lift."

The students were clean and tall, with short haircuts and well-pressed trousers and sports jackets. They were patronising and pleased to have him as a toy to display. He knew it. He minded. He ignored it as best he could. His long hair and his pretty clothes amused them, and they called him Robinson Flanders, like well-educated lads. They stopped at the lakeside city of Ostersund and decided to rest there for a couple of days, since they felt inexplicably tired. Jerry, on the other hand, felt much better.

By the time they reached Uppsala, Jerry had seduced both the young Swedes without either's knowing about his seduction of the other. They hardly realised they were so much in his power until he drove their Volvo off, leaving them in the city of the twin spires deciding not to say who had stolen their car.

The pickings were better in Eskilstuna, where he took up with a young female teacher who lived in the town and had hitched a lift from him. He began to straighten out. He half-regretted what he had done to the two students, but it had been an emergency. Now there was no panic, and the girl was proud of her delicate English lover—took him to parties in Eskilstuna and Stockholm. He got work reading the proofs of scientific papers published in English by a Stockholm academic press. It was light work and quite interesting and allowed him to have some new clothes made to his own specifications, buy some records, and even pay something towards the girl's rent. Her name was Una, and she was as tall, frail, and pale as he was, with long blonde hair and large light blue eyes. A pretty sight they made together.

They became very popular, Jerry Cornelius and Una Persson. The young people with whom they mixed—students, teachers, lecturers, mainly—began to imitate Jerry's styles; and he appreciated the compliment, began to feel much more at home.

By the way of a gesture of gratitude, after he had been in Eskilstuna for almost a year, he married Una. His earlier working-over had softened him more than he realised, and even though he'd recouped pretty well, he was almost in love with her and she with him. He played guitar with a semi-professional group who called themselves the Modern Pop Quintet—organ, bass, drums, alto—and made enough to pay his way like a good husband. The group was in demand and would soon go full-time. It was becoming like the old days, with the difference that he was not, as he'd been in London, remote and in the thick of crowds. Here he set the pace and got his name in *Svenskadagbladet* and the other papers. He shared equal space and appearances with the streams of analyses of what was rotten in the state of Europe. He was generally mentioned in these too. He'd become a symbol.

Drunk with nostalgia, publicity and hangers-on, he dreamed no more of Laplab and Miss Brunner and congratulated himself that he had found himself an island that could last him, with luck, until early middle age. He had taken the precaution of keeping the name the students had given him, Robinson Flanders.

Miss Brunner kept her data up to date. She read the papers in her private cavern-palace.

"He's become a little star."

15

So naturally the time came when Jerry's flat at Konigsgaten 5, Eskilstuna 2, Sweden, was visited. He came home from a session to find his pretty wife talking politely to Miss Brunner. They were both sitting on a couch sipping Una's excellent coffee. The room was sunny, small but pleasant, neat but not gaudy. He could see them from the front door. He put his guitar case in the hall and took off his coat of fine cord, put it on a hanger, hung it in the cupboard, and walked in, hand outstretched, to greet his old friend with a confident smile.

"Miss Brunner. You're looking well. A little tired, maybe—but well. How's the big project?"

"All but completed, Mr Cornelius."

He laughed. "But what do you do with it now?"

"There's the rub," she smiled, putting her white cup on the low table. She was dressed in a plain black sleeveless dress of good, rough stuff. She wore a perky hunting bowler on her long red hair and had a man's tightly rolled umbrella leaning beside her against the couch. Also beside her were a black leather briefcase and a pair of black gloves. Jerry had the feeling she had dressed for action, but he couldn't decide what sort of action and whether it directly involved him.

"Miss Brunner arrived about half an hour ago, Robby," Una explained softly, not quite sure now that she had acted wisely. "I told her I was expecting you shortly and she decided to wait."

"Miss Brunner was a close business acquaintance in the past." Jerry smiled at Miss Brunner. "But we have little in common now."

"Oh, I don't know." Miss Brunner returned the smile.

"You bitch," said Jerry. "Get out of here—back to your caves and your farce." He spoke rapidly in English, and Una missed the sense, though she seemed to get the message.

"You've found something to keep and protect at last, eh, Jerry? Albeit a travesty of something you lost?"

"Excuse me, Miss Brunner," said Una, somewhat coldly, in her husband's defence, "but why do you call Herr Flanders 'Jerry' and 'Mr Cornelius'?"

"Oh, they are old nicknames we used to have for him. A joke."

"Ha-ha! I see."

"Don't kid yourself, Miss Brunner," Jerry continued. "I'm fine."

"Then you're kidding yourself more than I'd guessed."

"Miss Brunner." Una got up tensely. "It seems I

made a mistake asking you to wait..."

Miss Brunner looked the tall girl up and down. One hand curled round the handle of the umbrella. She frowned thoughtfully.

"You and Professor Hira," she said. "A good pair of connections. I could go for you, dear."

Jerry moved in. He grabbed the umbrella and tried to snap it on his knee, failed and tossed it aside. He and Una stood over Miss Brunner, both with fists clenched. Miss Brunner shrugged impatiently.

"Jerry!"

"You'd better go back to Laplab," he said. "They need you there."

"And you—and this." She pointed at Una.

They were all breathing rapidly.

After a few moments of silence, Miss Brunner said, "Something's got to happen."

But Jerry waited, hoping for the almost inevitable break in tension that would weaken him but leave him out of the situation he could see Miss Brunner wanted to create.

The break didn't come. He did not glance at Una, afraid that she would look scared. Things were getting worse. Outside, the sun was setting. The break must come before the sun went down altogether.

The break didn't come. The tension increased. Una began to stir. "*Don't move!*" he shouted, not looking at her. Miss Brunner chuckled warmly.

The sun was down. Miss Brunner rose in the grey

light. She reached towards Una. Jerry's eyes filled with tears as he heard a deep, desperate sound come from his wife.

"*No!*" He moved forward, gripping Miss Brunner's arm as she took Una's quivering hand.

"It—is—necessary." Miss Brunner was in pain as his nails squeezed her flesh. "Jerry!"

"Ohhhhhh…" He took his hand off her arm.

Una stared at him helplessly, and he stared helplessly back.

"Come along," said Miss Brunner kindly but firmly, taking their hands and walking between them. "It is all for the best. Let us go and find Professor Hira." She led them from the flat to her waiting car.

PHASE

4

16

Five days later, sitting at a table on the terrace, warmed by artificial sunlight, nose and eye delighted by the profusion of flowers below, Jerry listened to Miss Brunner talking. It was a square table. On the other three sides of the square sat Miss Brunner, opposite Jerry; Una to his right; and Professor Hira to his left.

"Well," Miss Brunner was saying cheerfully, "we've all got to know one another pretty well, I think. It's amazing how quickly you settled in, Una."

Jerry glanced at his wife. He and she were the beauties here without a doubt, both elegant and delicate-seeming, she if anything paler than he. She smiled sweetly at Miss Brunner, who was patting her hand.

Professor Hira was reading a two-day-old *Aftonbladet*.

"The only snag as far as I can see is this business of the police believing that you kidnapped Mr and Mrs Cornelius, Miss Brunner," said the professor. "They have traced you to Lapland and must have found the outer signs of our establishment by now—this paper being out of date, you see."

"We do have defences, professor," she reminded him. "We can also seal off sections of the cave system if necessary. G-day is tomorrow, and after that we shall be finished within forty-eight hours. Even an all-out attack on Laplab, which isn't likely, would not be successful unless nuclear weapons were used; and I can't see the Swedes doing that, can you?"

"Would it not help if Mr Cornelius went out and spoke to the police searching the area?"

No, professor. Positively not. We cannot afford the slightest chance of losing Mr Cornelius at this stage."

"I feel flattered," said Jerry with a touch of bitterness. "On the other hand, you could let a few in and I could speak to them. They needn't come far—they wouldn't see DUEL at all."

"They wouldn't ask to. Don't forget, Mr Cornelius, that this land belongs to the Lapps under the protection of the Swedish government. They would be more than anxious to inspect us—particularly with the international situation in its present state and the Russian border close by. This is entirely the wrong time to hope to stall a nervous administration."

"I could go." Una spoke hesitantly.

Miss Brunner stroked the girl's hair. "I'm sorry, my darling, but I cannot trust you sufficiently. You are still a bit of a weakling, you know."

"I am sorry, Miss Brunner."

Jerry sat back, folding his arms. "What, then?"

"We can only hope for the best, as I said."

"There is another alternative." Jerry unfolded his arms. "We could send some men out to see what's going on, disguise the cave entrance, and, if they get the chance, lure any search party inside and dispose of it."

"That would not really solve the problem, but I will have it done." She rose and walked into the room, picking up a telephone. "Then at least we shall be able to question a few of them and find out exactly where we stand." She dialled a two-digit number and spoke some instructions into the mouthpiece.

"And now," she said pleasantly, beckoning them in, let us continue with our experiments. There is not much more to do, but there is little time before G-day."

"And then, I hope, you will tell us just what 'G-day' is, Miss Brunner. We are all very curious—though I have had a few hints, I think." Professor Hira laughed excitedly.

Vibrant, pulsing with enormous energies, flushed and light-headed, Jerry began to fold Una's clothes and place them on top of Professor Hira's. He felt totally fit, totally purified, totally alive. What was more, he felt replete, warm, at ease and at peace; like a great tiger in its prime, like a young god, he thought.

Miss Brunner lay on the bed. She gave him a knowing wink.

"How?" he said. "I didn't realise until it was over."

"It is power," she said luxuriously, "which many have potentially. You had it. It is natural, isn't it?"

"Yes." He lay down beside her. "But I've never heard of anything like it. Not physically, anyway."

"It is a trick. There's been a lot written in some form or other. The world's mythologies, particularly those closest to source, Hindu and Buddhist, are full of references. The secret was saved by over-interpretation. No-one, however dedicated, would believe in the literal truth."

"Ahhh."

"You regret nothing now?"

"I'm content."

"There is more to come. The connections brought us closer—"

The telephone was ringing.

She got up at once, walking swiftly from the room. More slowly, he followed her down to her office and entered as she replaced the receiver.

"Your plan worked. They have six policemen in the far cavern. They are talking to them. So far they have stalled them with a story about secret research sponsored by the Swedish government. We must go and talk to them now while they are still comparatively unsuspicious. Let's get dressed."

The policemen were polite but uncertain. They were also, Jerry noticed, armed with revolvers.

Miss Brunner smiled at them. "I am afraid I shall have to keep you here until we have checked with Stockholm," she said. "I am director of the establishment. Our work is highly secret. It is a great pity that you stumbled upon us—and inconvenient for you. I apologise."

Her foolproof Swedish, brisk and polite, made them relax a little.

"The area is not marked on our maps," said the oldest man, a captain. "It is usual to mark restricted areas."

"The work we are doing here is of maximum importance to Swedish security. We have guards on patrol, but we can't afford too many. Great numbers would attract attention."

"Of course. But in that case—" the captain paused, scratching his right hand with his left— "why locate such an establishment here? Why not in Stockholm or one of the other cities?"

"Could such vast natural caves be found in a city?" Miss Brunner waved a hand back at the cavern.

"Would it be possible for me to contact my superiors whilst you are checking with yours?"

"Out of the question. It is a puzzle to me that you are in this area."

"We believe that an Englishman and his wife—" He stopped short, staring for the first time at Jerry.

"Bugger me, why didn't we think of that?" said Jerry under his breath.

"But this is the Englishman," said the captain. His hand went to his holster.

"I was not brought here by force, captain," said Jerry

hurriedly. "I was contacted by your government to help…"

"That is unlikely, sir." The captain drew his revolver. "If that were the case, we should have been notified."

The four technicians who had brought the policemen in were unarmed, and so were Jerry and Miss Brunner. Apart from that, they were evenly matched, six against six. Miss Brunner's tough boys were out of earshot. Things looked dicey.

"An oversight surely, captain?" Miss Brunner's delivery was a bit rough now.

"I cannot believe that."

"I don't blame you, frankly," said Jerry, noting that only the captain had actually drawn his gun. The rest of them were still trying to catch up on what was happening.

Jerry's body was full of power.

He jumped for the gun. Two yards.

The gun went off once before he had disarmed the captain and covered the surprised policemen.

"You had better take over, Miss Brunner." Jerry's voice was thick. From inordinate energy he had sunk to exhaustion, dizziness. As she took the gun from him and covered the Swedes, he glanced down.

The bullet seemed to have entered his chest just above the heart. Loss of blood.

"Oh, no. I think I'm going to die. Mum?"

In the distance, Miss Brunner's tough boys came running. He heard Miss Brunner shouting orders, felt her arm supporting him. He seemed to be growing heavier and heavier, sinking through the stone.

Was it muffled gunfire he heard? Was it hopeful imagination that made him think he caught the sound of Miss Brunner's voice saying "There is still a chance—but we must work rapidly"?

His mass became greater than that of the stone, and he found he could walk through it with some difficulty, like pushing through air that had the consistency of thin, liquid tar.

He wondered if it were tar and if he would be found in millions of years perfectly preserved. He pushed on, knowing that this theory was stupid.

At length he emerged into the open, feeling light and fit.

He stood on a plain without a horizon. Far, far away he could make out a huge crowd of people gathered round a rostrum on which stood a single still figure. He heard the faint sound of voices and began to walk towards the crowd.

As he got closer, he recognised that the crowd, thousands strong, consisted of all Miss Brunner's scientists and technicians. Miss Brunner was on the rostrum addressing them.

No-one noticed him as he stopped at the back of the crowd and listened to her speech.

"You have all been waiting for the time when I would describe the ultimate purpose of DUEL. The biologists and neurologists may have guessed—and then decided that their guesses were too incredible and dismissed them. But they were right. I do not believe that our project can fail—unless Mr Cornelius should die, which now seems unlikely—"

Jerry was relieved.

"—and I believe in it sufficiently to be, with Mr Cornelius, the raw material."

Jerry worked out that he must be experiencing some sort of hallucination crossed with reality. The vision was dream; the words were actually being spoken. He tried to haul himself out of the dream but failed.

"DUEL's purpose was twofold, as you know. The first job was to feed it the sum total of human knowledge in one comprehensive integral equation. This was at last achieved three days ago, and I congratulate you.

"It is the second part that mystified most of you. The technical problem of how to feed this programme directly into a human brain was overcome with the help of notes donated by Dr Leslie Baxter, the psychobiologist. But what sort of brain could accept such a fantastic programme? That question is answered as I answer the question you have all been asking. DUEL's ultimate use is to satisfy an aim which, whether we realised it or not, has been the ultimate aim of all human endeavour since *Homo sapiens* first evolved. It is a simple aim and we are near achieving it. We have been working, ladies and gentlemen, to produce an all-purpose human being! A human being equipped with total knowledge, hermaphrodite in every respect—self-fertilising and thus self-regenerating—and thus immortal, re-creating itself over and over again, retaining its knowledge and adding to it. In short, ladies and gentlemen, we are creating a being that our ancestors would have called a god!"

The scene wavered, and Jerry heard the words less clearly.

"The conditions in modern Europe proved ideal for this project—ideal in every respect—and I believe that we succeed now or never. I have destroyed my notes. The necessary equipment has been constructed. Bring Mr Cornelius forward, please."

Jerry felt himself being lifted up and floated through the ghostly crowd.

He drifted behind Miss Brunner as she walked away towards a large oval metal chamber. Then they were inside it together, in darkness. Miss Brunner began to make gentle love to him. He felt her, closer and closer, drawing into him. It was like the dream he had had before.

Deliciously he felt himself merge with Miss Brunner, and he still wondered if this, too, were a dream inspired by his wound. And yet his body had breasts and two sets of genitals, and it seemed very real and very natural that this should be so. Then he felt tiny pricks of pain in his skull, and his memories and Miss Brunner's, his identity and hers, merged for a moment and then slowly dispersed until his mind was blanked out and DUEL began to do its stuff.

17

The technician looked sharply at his watch. Then he looked at the metal chamber and at the dials thereon. Every dial was now still. Slowly, a green light blinked on and off.

"This is it," said the technician crisply to another technician very like him.

The chamber had been rolled on casters close to DUEL. The great semicircle of the computer was joined by a huge semicircle of scientists and technicians, making a full circle.

A spotlight had been turned on the oval chamber. Scientists came forward to check that the indicators all registered correctly. They backed off, satisfied.

The middle-aged dietician who had won the honour through an elaborate draw spun the handle of the chamber.

• • • • •

A tall, naked, graceful being stepped out. It had Miss Brunner's hair and Mr Cornelius's eyes. Miss Brunner's predatory jaw was softened by Jerry's ascetic mouth. It was hermaphrodite and beautiful.

The scientists and technicians murmured in awe, and some of them began to clap and whistle. Others cheered and stamped.

"Hi, fans!" said Cornelius Brunner.

The cavern reverberated with a massive shout of exultation. The scientists and technicians capered about, clapping one another on the back, grinning, dancing.

They surged towards their smiling creation, lifted it high, and began to march round the computer singing a wordless victorious chant which became a christening name:

"Cor-nee-lee-us Ber-un-ner!"

Cornelius Brunner was making a big scene.

"Just call me Corn," it grinned, and it blew kisses to one and all.

Distantly at first, growing louder, a siren or two began to sound.

Corn cocked an ear. "The enemy is at our gates!" It pointed a slender finger towards the outer cavern. "Forward!"

Lifted on a rolling tide of its jubilant sycophants, many thousands strong, Cornelius Brunner sat on their shoulders as they flooded forward.

Across the great hall of the hot lake, up the slope towards the cave mouth, onward they moved, their roaring thunderous, their exhilarated bodies swift.

The door of the cave opened for them, and they rushed into the open air. Cornelius Brunner laughed as it rode their backs.

A small detachment of military was there. A few light guns and armoured cars.

The tide did not notice as the soldiers first backed away and then tried to run and then were engulfed, guns and cars and all, as the huge crowd coursed ahead in triumph.

Cornelius Brunner pointed to the south-west. "That way—to Finland first!"

The flow changed direction but not its speed, and away it went in its entirety.

It streamed over the border, it swarmed down the length of Finland, it flocked through Germany, and it gathered greater and greater numbers as it moved on, Cornelius Brunner high in the centre, encouraging it, urging it, praising it. The thousands became millions as the new messiah was borne across the continent, whole cities abandoned and the land crushed in its wake.

The vast swarm reached Belgium and, at its controller's behest, decimated Liège, depopulated Brussels, and carried half a nation with it when it crossed into France.

Its exuberant voice could be heard a hundred miles from Paris. The reverberation of its feet could be felt two hundred miles away. The aura of its presence rippled outward over the world.

The millions did not march along—they danced along. Their voice was one melodious song. Their densely packed mass covered fifty square miles or more, increasing all the time.

"To Paris!" cried Cornelius Brunner, and to Paris they went. Not once did they pause, aside from those who died from excitement.

Paris was passed, and its four remaining inhabitants gathered to watch the disappearing deluge.

"Unprecedented!" murmured the Chief of State, scratching his nose.

"Perhaps, perhaps," said his secretary.

The tide rolled on and roared through Rome, leaving the Pope, its sole resident, sunk in meditation and speculation. After some time, the Pope hurried from the Vatican Palace and caught up within an hour.

All the great cities of Italy. All the great cities of Spain and Portugal. All the cities of the Russian Empire.

And then, with a slight note of boredom in its voice, Cornelius Brunner gave the last order.

"To the sea!"

Down to the coast, onto the beaches, and tide met tide as the gigantic assemblage poured into the Black Sea.

Within six hours, only one head remained above water. Naturally, it was the head of Cornelius Brunner, swimming strongly towards a beach near Byzantium.

Cornelius Brunner stretched out on the well-churned sand and relaxed. The waves lapped the peaceful shore, and a few birds cruised the blue sky.

"This is the life," yawned Cornelius Brunner, whose skull contained the sum of human knowledge. "I think I might as well kip down here as anywhere."

Cornelius Brunner fell asleep, alone on an abandoned beach.

Night fell and morning followed, and it awoke.

"Where now?" it mused.

"To Normandy. There's some unfinished business."

"To Normandy, then, and the House of Cornelius."

It rose, flexed its body, turned, and loped inland over the quiet, deserted countryside.

TERMINAL DATA

The world's first all-purpose human being tucked the detonator under its arm and walked slowly backward, unwinding the wires that led to the cellar of the house. At a safe distance it set the box down and pulled up the plunger.

"Five!"

"Four!"

"Three!"

"Two!"

"One!"

Cornelius Brunner pressed the plunger, and the great fake Le Corbusier château split, flared and boomed. Gouts of flame and smoke erupted from it. The cliffside trembled, rubble flew, and the flames roared high, the black smoke hanging low and drifting down to obscure the village.

Arms folded, head set back, Cornelius Brunner contemplated the burning wreckage.

It sighed.

"That's that."

"Nice and tidy."

"Yes."

"What now?"

"I'm not sure. Perhaps the Middle East first."

"Or America?"

"No, not just yet, I think."

"I need some money. America might be the best place to get it."

"I feel like going East. There is still work to be done."

"The rainy season will have begun in Cambodia."

"Yes; I think I might as well walk, don't you?"

"There's plenty of time. Don't want to hurry."

Cornelius Brunner turned and looked down the slope of the cliff, turned again and looked back at the guttering house, looked out to sea, looked at the sky. "Ho hum."

A man, unshaven, clad in a ragged uniform, was panting up the slope. He called. "Monsieur—ah!"

"Monsieur-Madame," Cornelius Brunner corrected politely.

"Are you responsible for this destruction?"

"Indirectly, yes."

"There is still some law left in the land!"

"Here and there."

"I intend to arrest you!"

"I am beyond arresting."

"Beyond?" The official frowned.

Cornelius Brunner moved in. It began to stroke the official's arm.

"What's the time, monsieur? My watch has stopped."

The official glanced at his wrist, exposed by a tear in his sleeve. "Ah! Mine also!"

"Too bad." Cornelius Brunner looked into his eyes.

A sweet and gentle smile crossed his lips, and he flushed in ecstatic fascination while Cornelius Brunner removed his trousers.

The trousers were flung away. Cornelius Brunner turned the official round, smacked his bottom, gave him a gentle pat on the back, and sent him running back down the slope. He ran joyously, the smile still on his face, his ragged jacket and shirt-tails flapping.

A moment later, the world's first all-purpose human being strode eastward, whistling.

"A tasty world," it reflected cheerfully. "A very tasty world."

"You said it, Cornelius!"